TIME TO DIE

A DI SCOTT BAKER CRIME THRILLER

JAY NADAL

INKUBATOR
BOOKS

Published by Inkubator Books
www.inkubatorbooks.com

ISBN (eBook): 978-1-83756-039-4
ISBN (Paperback): 978-1-83756-040-0
ISBN (Hardcover): 978-1-83756-041-7

Previously published by the author as Greed.

PROLOGUE

He searched the darkness; no one was watching. With his dark clothing, he'd taken every precaution to blend into the background. He'd been travelling light, his wardrobe limited, his possessions few and far between.

The town had a different feel in the early hours of the morning. The streets were empty. A hazy mist drifted, adding an unwelcome chill to his skin and wrapping itself around everything else like an invisible cloak.

The locals once referred to this street as Restaurant Street, but a succession of countrywide recessions had put an end to the vibrancy it once enjoyed. Soaring rents and fewer diners had claimed many victims. Now all that was left were low-end pizza and kebab shops, Chinese supermarkets and a dozen or so boarded-up shops.

The road had a shallow incline from the seafront to Western Road, three hundred yards farther up. During the day, the busy road would be packed with holidaymakers and locals who used it as a cut-through between the seafront and main road. At this hour, it was abandoned to the ghostly shadows and emptiness of the night. His only company was a solitary fox wandering from one side of the road to the other in search of food.

In a matter of a few weeks his world had imploded, and now it was payback time. He'd been following the same man for a few days, spending hours moving from location to location, building a picture of his routine. This was supposed to be the easy bit, but he hated waiting. The voice raging inside his head had no patience.

Despite convincing himself that it would soon be over, what happened next terrified him. But it needed to be done. It was one thing to stand in the shadows but another to kill. He knew a killer needed nerves of steel, an unforgiving nature and a cold-blooded determination. A killer needed to separate intention from emotion, but was that him? Could he go through with it?

He found the notion hard to accept; he was just a boy in a man's body after all.

A constant stream of traffic cruised along the seafront, and a mass of pissed revellers spilled out of the bars and restaurants in neighbouring roads. Somewhere to his right he heard shouting. To his left, the salty sea air carried in on the gentle breeze, accompanied by the sound of waves lapping against the pebble beach. Frustration gnawed at him that the town never slept.

Sirens wailed in the distance. They weren't coming for him; he was sure of that.

He was in no hurry. It was a matter of waiting for the right opportunity, the right moment to strike. He knew the precise movement of his targets and knew the right time and place to expedite their journey to hell.

His eyes darted every which way in the gloom. The man he'd been waiting for appeared, accompanied by several associates. They were in the final throes of saying goodbye and talking in hushed conversations beneath the yellow hue of a street light. His head throbbed as his body stiffened with tension.

A few final handshakes followed before the man threw his cigarette to the ground, extinguishing it with a short, sharp twist of his shoe.

The killer smiled, knowing that within moments, the man would meet a similar swift demise.

A final farewell and the target walked away, passing several doorways, oblivious to his fate. The smell of stale cigarette smoke carried in the light breeze. It was a nauseating aroma that turned his stomach.

He stepped out from the shadows and trailed his victim. He needed to strike now. It was the farthest point from the nearest street light and gave him the best cover.

He'd practised his approach many times, mastered the art of following without detection. He quickened his pace, his heart thumping inside his chest. His breath grew shallow and rapid; his eyes widened with fear. The first few beads of sweat formed on his forehead.

He reached into the back of his jeans and felt the cold steel of his knife press against his skin. He pulled it out, the sharp edge glinting in the moonlight.

He'd given his choice of weapon considerable thought; it needed to inflict maximum damage on his target. There was no margin for error; there was no turning back. If he hesitated, there was a risk the target could turn and strike back.

The target must have sensed his approach because he did turn. His shoulders hunched in defence, but he wasn't quick enough to react. The last thing his victim saw, terror in his eyes, was the glint of the knife as it plunged into his neck like a hot knife through butter. The killer knew that with enough force, the strike would render the victim immobile, unable to make a sound, and his life would be extinguished in a matter of moments.

The victim raised his arms in a fruitless act of self-defence, the life already draining out of him. Too weak now, he collapsed to his knees and fell face down, his head hitting the cold pavement with a sickening thud and crack.

The killer tugged the knife out of his victim. Remnants of flesh entangled in the serrated teeth, and as the wet skin tore, blood spurted out to form a dark shiny pool around the victim's head. The victim gurgled and coughed as blood collected in his throat.

One final act needed to be completed.

The killer prised open the victim's mouth and did what he had to do.

His job was done, just as he'd planned in his mind. He'd been clever, been careful to cover his tracks and leave no clues. Drawing on all his strength, he dragged the lifeless body off the street and over to a collection of bins. There, he hoisted the body up.

"Fucker," he cursed as he lost his grip on the blood-soaked clothing. He hadn't considered how hard it would be to lift a corpse into a large, industrial waste bin. But somehow he managed it.

With the victim stowed away, the killer was confident he'd be safely tucked up in bed by morning when the bastard was found.

New anger coursed through his veins, causing his heart to burst through his chest.

It was a bittersweet moment. Deep within the pit of his stomach, sadness still reigned, shrouding him like a dark, menacing mist. His eyes narrowed. His jaw tightened. His brow furrowed, like a child who had just been chastised.

Ever since he was a child, his frequent bouts of sadness went hand-in-hand with daily humiliation. He was made an example of to the other kids. His body was used repeatedly for sexual gratification by those who were supposed to be protecting him.

As he stood there now, history repeated itself. His underwear and jeans were yet again warm with urine; tears flowed from his eyes, blurring his vision.

Taking a life couldn't replace what had been stolen from him, but he felt satisfied with the retribution it had delivered.

1

Somewhere in the hazy distance Scott heard his phone ringing. The sound of House of Pain was too upbeat for this time of the morning. Even though he loved "Jump Around", it had been the butt of jokes in the office. He didn't care; it was a nostalgic track from his university days, at the Gloucester nightclub near the seafront.

The sun crept in through the slats in his bedroom blinds, casting strips of light and darkness across his room that danced on the wall. He'd been meaning to get proper curtains to darken his room for some time and was starting to regret not doing it sooner.

He closed his eyes in the hope that the sun would go away and the ringing would stop. Then there was silence.

Ah, peace at last.

The peace lasted only moments before his phone sprang into action again, doing its damned hardest to rob him of any chance of a few extra minutes in bed. This time he knew that it was either a persistent sales call or something official. As he glanced at his alarm clock on his bedside table, the red digits glowed a bright six forty a.m.

This was the last thing he needed after having done seven straight days on. His last shift had finished at eleven p.m. the night before, after his team had finished processing prisoners from an earlier operation.

He had realised early in his CID role that shift work had its advantages; being woken on a day off wasn't one of them. Eight-hour shifts were nothing more than a luxury and a distant dream these days. As a sergeant, his DI often reminded him that criminals never did a thirty-five-hour week, nor did they only work weekdays.

It was a mindset he'd adopted due to modern-day policing being squeezed from every angle. Political pressures to increase crime detection rates, whilst introducing greater efficiency, came with smaller budgets and fewer officers to do the same amount of work. Budgetary cuts across the force had also led to a reduction in his team.

Once, he'd had the luxury of two detective sergeants and five detective constables. He was now down to less than half that number, but the caseload remained the same. Consequently, his team had the unenvied task of juggling every precious hour on shift. More than half of their time was tied up with filling out forms – there were forms for everything, and Scott hated the sight of them. He wanted to get on with what he signed up to do, catch criminals.

He stumbled out of bed, getting his bearings, knocking over a half-empty glass of Jack Daniel's that sat on the floor. It served as a poignant reminder of the night before and his fruitless attempt to stop his mind whirring and escape into a deep slumber.

He swayed as his half-closed eyes sought to focus and locate the source of his annoyance. He felt like crap, his stomach burning from the punishment he'd given it last night. His back refused to straighten up, his knees creaked as he moved, and his eyes were sticky with sleep gunk.

Scott reached for the phone on his dresser and looked at the screen, willing it to come into focus. He moved the phone closer and away until his vision cleared. DC Mike Wilson flashed up as the caller ID. He answered it.

"Mike, this'd better be good; what's up?" he said, with a hoarse and gravelly voice.

Slight hesitance on Mike's part caused Scott to worry. "Erm, guv, we've got a body; it's a nasty one. I know it's your day off, but DCI Harvey needs you to come over because she's away for the weekend. She's heading home now but won't be back until this evening."

Scott groaned. The DCI was away on a boozy weekend with chums, and nothing short of an apocalyptic disaster would bring her back to the office.

"Okay, Mike, give me thirty minutes, and I'll be there. Where is it?"

"It's in Preston Street, the Kings Road end, guv. SOCO are on-site."

"Blimey, they're quick off the mark. Do I need to skip brekkie?"

"Probably wise, guv, unless you want to see it in reverse," Mike fired back. "You'll see what I mean when you get here."

2

Within ten minutes Scott had thrown on a pair of dark-grey trousers, a white shirt and a pair of black brogues before heading off in his black Audi A3. It was his pride and joy, and he preferred to use his own car instead of one of the CID pool cars when out on police business.

Scott lived in Hove about three miles from the city centre of Brighton on the south coast. Hove was a much quieter residential area than its bigger, more bustling neighbour. Brighton, a popular seaside resort, was often referred to as London-by-the-sea. Only a short fifty-minute train journey into London, many workers escaped to Brighton after a hard day in the capital. Consequently, house prices were comparable to those in London, which had led to a rich and vibrant mix of inhabitants, from city professionals to locals and students.

Scott had loved Brighton and its buzz from the minute he'd arrived at the University of Brighton.

After graduating at twenty-three, he'd returned to his home town of Brentwood in Essex, soon joining Essex Police.

He'd steadily fast-tracked his way up the ladder. At the age of thirty-two, he joined the Sussex force CID as a detective sergeant – a promotion that still annoyed several time-served officers. It was also where he'd met his wife, Tina.

He and Tina, both sporty, had first bumped into each other on the London-to-Brighton cycle run. It had been the start of a wonderful relationship. Sunny weekends were spent sitting on the beach relaxing or playing air hockey in the arcades on Palace Pier. Their competitive streaks never took long to come out.

Scott had loved nothing more than wandering hand in hand with Tina around The Lanes, enjoying the culture, discovering small bistros and boutique shops... All wonderful memories that brought him happiness and sadness in equal measure.

He turned left onto Kingsway and drove along the coast road. There was something serene and relaxing about the sea view, the smell of salt air and the constant chatter from seagulls that floated on the thermals whilst scavenging for discarded chips and other takeaway delicacies.

Today wasn't any different. There was sharpness in the air, and winter still had its claws firmly dug in. The chill, together with a low setting sun, meant the mornings and evenings were crisp and occasionally frosty. However, daytime temperatures could often creep into the low double figures. To others around the country, the chilly weather would be enough to dampen spirits. Brightonians, on the other hand, were a hardy bunch and embraced it like the tonic it was.

It wasn't long before Scott saw the flashing blue lights and the blue and white police cordon tape fluttering in the breeze. Traffic had dropped to a snail's pace as drivers rubbernecked, hoping to satisfy their perverse curiosity by catching a glimpse of someone's misfortune.

Scott parked up behind a squad car and stepped out. He was greeted by a crowd of nosey spectators with nothing better to do than watch the spectacle unfolding.

Why are people fascinated with the misfortune of others?

With gritted teeth, Scott pushed through the crowd before ducking under the tape.

3

Preston Street was narrow and hemmed in by four-storey Regency-style buildings, many in desperate need of renovation. Paint curled at the edges and flaked off the walls. The windows were grubby and gritty. It was fair to say that the street was a far cry from its neighbour, Regency Square, that boasted magnificent, grade-two-listed buildings. Impressive well-maintained cream exteriors housed exquisite, generous-sized apartments and boutique hotels.

Out towards the seafront and beyond lay the ruins of the once magnificent West Pier, now nothing more than a few iron support structures jutting out from the seabed, resembling a decapitated, battered and twisted metal skeleton. Scott reflected on the damage that had been caused to the pier during the great storm of 1987. It had wreaked havoc across the city, levelling thousands of trees and bringing down power lines. A subsequent storm and fire fifteen years later had delivered the final blow to the pier, causing its collapse into a watery grave.

The crime scene had been cordoned off with police tape.

To protect the area, a scene guard was on duty to monitor the cordon. Their key tasks were to protect the scene from contamination by onlookers, preserve the integrity of exhibits and account for the presence and movement of all personnel within the designated area. The scene guard on this occasion was PC Willits, who lifted the blue and white tape when Scott approached.

As Scott ducked under the tape marking the edge of the crime scene, Willits gave him a courteous, "Good morning, sir."

Scott stared at her as he signed into the scene log. "Is it, Constable?"

Willits shifted uncomfortably and looked away. Scott walked off, instantly berating himself for being so abrupt to the young PC, but given that he was still numb and fatigued, he wasn't ready to be courteous. He grabbed his morning coffee, a fix that soon jolted him awake and turned him into someone closely resembling a human being.

He took a protective suit pack from a brown box beside the PC and kitted up.

SOCO were present, all kitted up in identical white paper protective suits, masks that robbed them of any identity, and blue shoe coverings. From where Scott stood, it was hard to tell who was male or female.

Scott spotted DC Mike Wilson. He was dressed in the same attire – but no mask – and stood close to the second of two white tents, erected about twenty feet apart, to protect and preserve the crime scene.

Mike was a stocky five feet eleven inches, with an expanding waistline. He bore the hallmarks of his ex-army days with a flat-top crew cut, a multitude of tattoos that catalogued his time in the forces. His no-bullshit, often crude, northern English accent made him unlike most police officers a person would usually meet.

The army instilled loyalty and fortitude in its soldiers, which Mike had in abundance. He was methodical, precise, and more importantly, if the shit hit the fan, he was by Scott's side. Mike was an asset to the team and someone Scott had relied on many times. Mike didn't always play by the rules, sometimes resorting to unorthodox tactics and "gentle persuasion", as Mike put it.

Despite Scott being his superior, he'd turned a blind eye to Wilson's approach whenever the end justified the means.

Scott peered into the smaller of the two tents before joining Mike, who looked up from his notes.

"Morning, guv. He's inside this tent," he said, indicating with his head. "It's not pretty."

He sighed. "A corpse never is – unless you're into that type of stuff."

"Of course, guv. Can't get enough of them myself," Mike fired back, a reference to his days as an army sniper.

Scott took a deep breath and peered in through the unzipped entrance. He wasn't keen to step in for many reasons; the first being he didn't want to disturb the crime scene until SOCO were finished, and secondly, the thought of getting up close and personal with a stiff wasn't something he needed whilst his stomach still felt fragile.

There were three crime scene officers inside the tent. One was taking photos of the body, another was inspecting the waste bin whilst standing on a two-step ladder, and the third was doing a systematic sweep on a section of pavement. Scott entered and was instantly greeted by the smell of death. It was a scent that got into his nostrils and lingered.

The body was prone on the floor. The man's white shirt was now dark red bordering on black, due to the dried blood. Evident to all was the severe trauma inflicted on the neck region. It was hard to determine if the head had been partially severed from the angle it was resting. The mouth hung wide open, expressing the shock of the victim's final moments.

Something caught Scott's attention. He got closer to what appeared to be a paper-like substance stuffed into the victim's mouth.

A gag?

4

Mike said, "The pathologist has just arrived, guv. Abby and Raj are en route to help out and should be here in the next few minutes."

Scott followed Mike across the pavement to take a wider look at the scene. "Good stuff. So what have we so far, Mike?"

"He was found over there in the industrial bin this morning, guv," Mike pointed out, "by some workmen who are renovating the West Beach Hotel on the corner. Scared them shitless, from what I can gather. After the preliminaries, SOCO removed his body so they could analyse the bin and the victim. Uniform are with the workmen inside the hotel now.

"We found a wallet in his suit jacket; usual stuff in there like money, cards, pictures of the deceased with a female, and driver's licence all with the same name. The victim appears to be Edward Stone. SOCO will do a prints match later to confirm against any prints on file."

Scott nodded whilst looking around the street.

"What do we know about him, any next of kin?"

"I checked the PNC, and if it's the same guy, he's the

owner of the Phoenix nightclub just over there, and his address is a flat in Fourth Avenue, Hove. He lives there with his girlfriend, Vicky Bright. He's known to the police, guv. He's got previous convictions for assault and fraud."

Scott raised a brow in reflection.

As Mike continued to update Scott on the situation, the crime scene manager and senior SOCO, Matt Allan, walked over to interrupt them. Matt was in charge of the scientific services team and, on complex and more serious cases, was usually present to oversee the whole crime scene and the allocation of his team's tasks.

Scott had worked with Matt often, and they enjoyed a good working relationship. Matt was always impeccably dressed. There was never a shirt tail hanging out the back of his trousers, or a loose tie with a top button undone, or even the slightest trace of a stain on his shirts. That attention to detail distilled down to his work ethic and professional demeanour. He was precise and to the point in conversations, his crime scene reports and approach to life.

"Morning, Scott," Matt butted in.

Scott grunted. "Why is everyone so damn chirpy and upbeat this morning?"

He wasn't normally this grumpy. He had decent social skills and a natural ability to get along with anyone. He also wasn't a typical senior officer. He was happy mixing and got along with those in uniform as well as his CID colleagues. Scott had very few hang-ups; didn't smoke or drink, apart from the odd social drink, but that slipped on a few occasions. He kept fit and enjoyed watching weird programmes like *Great Continental Railway Journeys*, or David Attenborough's latest soothing commentary about the marvels of some exotic creature that no one had heard of.

Today was different though. The day before had been

March 18, a day he dreaded. A date that brought him sorrow and anger.

"A little touchy this morning, are we? One too many lemonades last night?" Matt winked.

"I've had better, mate. Just shattered and got a lot on my mind. Everyone's far too bloody cheery for my liking, that's all."

Matt smiled and nodded. "Well, you'll be pleased to know that my team has nearly finished. We got some partial footprints in the dried blood inside both tents. The victim had a silver curb necklace with a matching silver ring hanging off it. The ring was engraved 'Eddy and Vicky, 4th Sept.' We're waiting on a low-loader to take away the bin for further analysis, and we'll get our report over to you in the next forty-eight hours."

"Forty-eight hours?" Scott fired back. "You're taking the piss... Make it twenty-four hours. We're going to have the press crawling over this soon. It's a hot one."

Scott nodded in the direction of the police cordon, where crowd numbers had swelled. Some were pointing their phones in his direction. No doubt their work would end up on YouTube later. If the crowd was expecting a glamorous scene matching that from a TV crime scene show, then they were going to be sorely disappointed.

"Twenty-four hours, right?" Scott said again more forcefully.

Matt shrugged and nodded in submission.

5

"The victim was stabbed in the neck, and the pathologist will confirm this was the cause of death," Crime Scene Manager Matt Allan said. "It was probably a large knife considering the size of the wound. We haven't found the murder weapon." He pointed to the smaller tent. "It looks like he was attacked over there. And the trail of blood suggests he was dragged to the second location and tossed into the bin."

Matt reached into a box by his feet. "What's interesting is this..." He pulled out a clear plastic evidence bag with three bloodstained twenty-pound notes. "We found them stuffed inside the victim's mouth. That's a first for me."

"Guess he was stuffed after a night out," Mike quipped.

"Funny..." Scott scowled as he pinched his forehead to calm his pounding headache.

Both Mike and Scott leant in to inspect the bag.

Matt said, "We'll take a closer look back at the lab and see if there are any surviving prints."

Scott nodded. "Okay, do your best, and I'll catch up with you later."

"Will do." Matt picked up the box and headed back to his van.

Scott turned to Wilson. "Mike, can you brief Abby and Raj when they arrive? I'm going to see what the pathologist has to say." Mike nodded as Scott left him and walked over to the larger tent. As he was approaching the tent, the pathologist, Cara Hall, stepped out.

Cara was thirty-eight years old, one year older than Scott, tall at five feet seven inches, with dark brown hair that was always tied up high in a ponytail. She wore outfits that suited her hourglass figure, wore very little makeup and had a natural English rose look about her. The opposite to what one might expect a stereotypical pathologist to look like: sombre, professional attire, perhaps a look of seriousness on her face indicating her clinical, meticulous and obsessive nature.

But Hall was so far removed from that. She had a cheeky sense of humour, which helped balance the seriousness of her work.

Cara removed her face mask and spotted Scott walking over to her.

She smiled broadly. "Detective Inspector Baker, we have the pleasure of your company on this crisp morning."

Great, another cheerful soul.

"Good to see you too, Dr Hall. What are your preliminary thoughts?"

"Well, upon initial inspection, he's definitely dead," she said with another smile.

Scott rolled his eyes and shook his head in mock despair. "Now that you're sure of that, any idea on time of death?"

"Hard to say for sure, but I'd estimate between four to six hours ago. We have primary flaccidity, as we can still move the body. Rigor mortis hasn't spread yet, but that may also be due to the ambient temperature slowing its onset. It was cooler in the early hours of the morning," she said with a shrug.

Scott nodded in agreement with her conclusion.

Cara continued, "The mortuary boys are here and ready to take him away, and I'll arrange for a special post-mortem for later this afternoon if that suits you? Can you stay awake long enough for that?" She raised one brow.

"I'll be there. Cause of death?"

"From my initial inspection, it's one open wound to the neck with a sharp instrument. I'll be able to confirm that when I check the rest of the body this afternoon." She glanced at her watch, her face serious for a moment. "Is that all for the moment? I need to head off to a suspected suicide in Peacehaven."

"Yes of course, thanks for coming out so quickly, Dr Hall, I'll see you later. Let me know what time."

Cara nodded. "I'll get one of the technicians to let you know,"

Scott walked back to the edge of the cordon where Mike was standing talking to PC Willits.

"Mike, change of plan, I'm going to grab a coffee from around the corner and then head over to the address we have and see if I can find out more. If it is the same man who lives there, I'd like to get him formally ID'd this morning, before the post-mortem. Get on the blower to Abby and tell her to meet me outside the apartment and see if we can get a family liaison officer to meet us there. When Raj gets here, I want you both to get full statements from the workmen. Then get a few uniforms to go door to door, to see if anyone saw or heard anything between two and four this morning. I'll meet you back at the station later."

Mike nodded. "Will do, guv."

Scott removed his protective clothing before heading back to his car. No sooner had he started to walk off, he stopped, paused for a moment, looked down at the ground, then turned back to where PC Willits was standing on cordon duty.

"Constable, I'm sorry for being so sharp with you earlier. Bad morning," he said with a tight-lipped smile.

Clearly taken aback by the apology, the constable was slow to reply, but finally blurted, "No need to apologise, sir, but thanks."

6

Fourth Avenue in Hove was a clean, wide, tree-lined street that had several properties with impeccably well-maintained frontages. Many had small walled front gardens with an array of low-maintenance shrubs, flowerpots, and fashionable slate features. Balconies finished off their look, which took advantage of the sea views.

Most of the three-storey buildings were luxury mansion flats. There was residents' parking on either side of the road, plus an additional double row of parking down the middle.

Scott parked up close to the address given for Edward Stone. DS Abby Trent waited close to the apartment.

Abby had been with Brighton CID for two years. Scott considered her a real grafter. She was reliable, conscientious and took a methodical approach to her work. He thought of her as a friend and colleague.

Abby had run in the London Marathon as part of the Sussex Police team on several occasions, coming in as the third-fastest female officer in Sussex. She was proud of her achievement, a testament to the many hours she devoted to keeping fit, whenever her shifts allowed.

At five feet four inches, with a slight frame, mousy blonde, shoulder-length hair and athletic build, many in the force often underestimated Abby's capabilities. But as a single mum of two juggling an active lifestyle and long hours on the job, she demonstrated a strong motivation to succeed and hated failure.

That was why Scott's description of her was so apt.

He studied the front of the building. "I'm assuming this is where the victim lived? We need confirmation from his girlfriend, if she's in. Have we got a family liaison officer free to join us?"

"Yes, guv. PC Andrea Smith is joining us. In fact, she's coming up the road right now." Abby nodded past Scott's shoulder.

He looked back. "Oh, good."

Andrea was in her late thirties, with jet-black short dyed hair. Her calm, reassuring manner had often helped the bereaved to get through very difficult and dark times. She had dressed casually. Though she was there in an official capacity, she didn't want the formality of a suit to create a barrier when her role was to be a supportive friend.

Scott had every bit of confidence in her. Constable Andrea Smith was well versed in these situations, and Scott had found her to be an invaluable support when dealing with family members.

Once Andrea joined them, he nodded at her.

Scott rang the buzzer for the first-floor flat. They waited a moment, and when there was no answer, Scott held the buzzer down again for a few seconds longer.

The intercom crackled before a voice with a strong cockney accent answered. "Hold your horses. I heard you the first time. Who is it?"

"Is that Vicky Bright?" Scott asked.

"Who wants to know?" the voice replied sharply.

Scott raised a brow at Abby before replying, "It's Brighton CID. May we come in for a moment?"

A pause followed, which Scott took as an indication that the woman was either weighing up what to say or wondering why they had turned up on her doorstep. Either way, the wait was starting to annoy him.

The door buzzer finally sounded, and the lock opened with a sharp click. They entered the hallway that led to a ground-floor flat to the left. A set of stairs to the right led up to the first floor. The walls were painted a light blue, with cream-coloured marble floor tiles covering the full length of the hallway.

Abby looked around, admiring the dark, highly polished rosewood handrail that continued the luxury theme clearly evident from the outside.

Scott felt certain that if their man lived here, then this was no ordinary mugging gone wrong. Perhaps it was a feud between rival small-time gang members.

Flat two on the first floor was halfway down the corridor. Scott knocked on the door and waited for it to be answered.

A few moments later, the soft sound of footsteps could be heard on the other side of the door, and then a pause, which Scott took to mean Vicky Bright was peeking through the spy hole in the door.

A woman in her early to mid-thirties opened the door, but she could have been younger. It was hard to tell. Vicky had the type of leathery skin suggesting she'd spent too much time in the sun. She had either just been away or had regular tanning sessions. Scott suspected the latter, judging from her not-so-healthy orange glow.

Vicky was wearing white Converse trainers, a pair of tight blue jeans that fitted her petite five-foot-one-inch frame and an orange top with a deep V-neck. Her dark roots were visible through her blonde hair.

All three officers held up their warrant cards.

"I'm Detective Inspector Baker," Scott said. "This is Detective Sergeant Abby Trent, and this is Police Constable Andrea Smith. May we come in for a few moments?"

Vicky Bright didn't say a word. She looked back and forth between the three visitors on her doorstep before waving them in and closing the door. She silently led them through to the lounge, which was on the right of the hallway next to the master bedroom.

Directly opposite the front door was a slightly smaller bedroom. With its door open, Scott could see a balcony overlooking the main road. To the left was a third bedroom, main bathroom and kitchen. The apartment was immaculately decorated, with tall ceilings and small chandeliers. Period features had been restored, like the ceiling covings, ornate fireplaces and deep, eight-inch skirtings.

Scott and Andrea sat down on a dark caramel-coloured velour sofa that swallowed them up. Abby and Vicky sat in matching armchairs.

Clearly unsure as to the reason for the visit, Vicky sat with her arms folded in front of her chest.

As Scott looked around, he noticed the walls were painted in two tasteful colours. The lower half had a similar caramel colour to the sofa, with a contrasting light cream applied to the upper half. The luxurious carpets were deep pile. Expensive furniture pieces were dotted around the room. No expense had been spared decorating this apartment.

"What's this about?" Vicky snapped.

7

"Can we confirm that you know Edward Stone?" asked Abby.

Vicky paused whilst scanning the faces of the three officers, looking unsure of what to say. Eventually, she gave them a slight nod.

"And are you in a relationship with him?" Abby continued.

"Yes, he's my fiancé... Why, what's this about? He ain't here, if that's what you wanna know."

"When's the last time you saw him?" Scott asked.

"I saw him about seven p.m. last night before he went off to the club. He ain't back yet." Her voice had a gravelly tone from years of chain-smoking.

"Would he normally be back by now, Vicky?" Scott asked.

"Usually he's back by four a.m. after the club's closed and he's done the takings. But sometimes he stays out all night if he goes to the casino or plays poker."

Scott spotted a few silver-framed photos with Vicky in several poses with a man, who had his arm around her.

"Is that him in the pictures above the fireplace?" he asked.

"Yes, that's my Eddie. They were taken when we was on holiday in the Bahamas last year. It was where we got engaged. Fourth of September on the beach."

Abby and Scott exchanged a brief glance; Scott gave her a small nod.

Vicky's brow furrowed as concern lines etched her forehead. She wrung her hands together. "What's this about?" Her voice grew louder.

Family liaison officer PC Andrea Smith leant forward. "Is there anyone you can call who can come and be with you?"

Vicky blinked in confusion. "My friend Michelle lives up the road. Please, what's going on? You're starting to freak me out. What's Eddy done now?"

"Could you ask Michelle to come over, please?" Andrea insisted softly.

"Yeah, I will when you tell me what's going on."

"I'm sorry to say, but we've found a body, and we have reason to believe it's Edward Stone," said Andrea.

Vicky's eyes widened, her jaw dropped, and her chest heaved. "No... no... not my Eddy."

She gripped the armrests so hard, Scott couldn't tell if she was going to scream or cry.

He had been in many situations like this before, and each one was different. On hearing about the sudden death of a loved one, relatives often expressed their emotions in different ways. Some would cry hysterically, some would whimper or go quiet, whilst others would fly into a fit of rage. Scott had drummed into his officers the importance of being prepared to deal with any type of reaction.

In this instance, Vicky was becoming increasingly agitated.

"Eddy, no... no... no, babes. Please, not my Eddy," was all the officers heard before Vicky jumped from her chair. In confusion, she looked left, then right, her hands wringing an imaginary towel, her breathing laboured. She began to hyperventilate.

Vicky let out a high-pitched scream loud enough to be heard outside. Next came the sobbing. She sat down heavily in the chair, her head in her hands, crying to herself.

Andrea got up from her chair and knelt beside Vicky and offered her a tissue, which was gratefully accepted.

"What... what happened to him? Are you sure it's him?" Vicky said, desperation in her voice. Her eyes searched the officers' faces, willing this to be a dream, hoping the police had got it horribly wrong and it was a case of mistaken identity. Scott had seen it all before.

He replied, "I'm sorry to have to tell you, but we believe that Edward was the victim of a violent assault."

The shock engulfed Vicky again. She looked up to the ceiling, perhaps hoping for divine intervention. Tears streaked her face, and her hands remained clenched on her lap.

Andrea left the room in search of the kitchen to make Vicky a strong cup of sweet tea. This was her usual MO during these visits.

Scott continued, "We found a wallet in the suit jacket of the victim, and the driving licence appears to match the victim and the pictures of Edward you have there on your mantelpiece. He had a ring on a chain, which was engraved –"

Vicky finished his sentence. "Eddy and Vicky 4th Sept..." Her voice trailed off, and she stared into emptiness. She snapped back to attention. "What happened to him?"

"We won't be one hundred per cent sure until the post-mortem is done, but it appears that he was stabbed."

"Oh Jesus..." Her bottom lip quivered.

Abby asked, "There's never a good time to ask, and I'm sorry for asking you now, but for completeness, we'll need to take a statement from you and also ascertain your whereabouts last night between two and four a.m. Andrea can take you to the station when you're ready, or we can do it here."

Vicky's eyes widened. "Why do I have to do that? I was in bed like I normally am at that time of night."

Abby continued, "Nevertheless, Vicky, we have to because you were Edward's partner. We also need to search the flat and formally identify the body."

Andrea returned and handed Vicky the mug of tea. Appearing defeated and weary, she took it from her.

After a moment she replied, "Do whatever you have to."

Scott said, "We'll leave you with Andrea for the time being." He motioned to Abby.

Outside the block on the street, Abby looked up at the apartment.

"She reacted like he was some kind of angel," she muttered.

"Well, she clearly loved him."

She looked at Scott. "Loved him or loved the lifestyle?"

"Who rattled your cage?"

"Did you see the bundle of cash on the table in the hall as we walked in?"

"I did; all fifty-pound notes, from what I could see." Scott estimated there must have been in excess of a grand sitting there. "Not sure I know many who leave a wad of cash like that lying around."

Abby nodded. "Exactly."

8

Abby headed back to the crime scene whilst Andrea stayed behind to take Vicky's statement at the apartment followed by her formal identification of the body.

Scott had received a text from the mortuary earlier confirming that the post-mortem would take place at three p.m. That would give him enough time to grab a bite to eat. He headed for Redeli, one of his favourite sandwich bars in Ship Street, where he grabbed his usual of chicken, tomato and avocado in a freshly cooked brown baguette.

SHORTLY AFTER THREE FORTY-FIVE P.M., Scott pulled up at the mortuary in Lewes Road and parked in the visitors' bay. He never looked forward to this part of an investigation: there was something macabre about watching a body being taken apart. A mortuary technician showed him into an anteroom with a glass-panelled wall that overlooked the main inspection room.

Pathologist Cara Hall was working on the body when she was made aware of the inspector's arrival by the technician assisting her.

"You won't see much from there, Detective Inspector." Her voice burst through the intercom.

That was what I was hoping for. I must remember to drive even slower next time.

Scott reluctantly got up and put on the required robes and a paper mask. Each stage took him closer to the inevitable stench of death.

He walked into the room. Edward Stone lay naked on the table with the preliminaries like his weight and height already noted. Cara was engrossed in a closer examination of Stone's neck. She had cut and peeled back the skin from around the wound to expose the muscular, skeletal and organ substructures.

"Thanks for scheduling this PM so quickly, Dr Hall. What have you got so far?"

"Quite a lot, actually. As you can see, he has hypostatic discolouration on his right shoulder and on the right-hand side of his face. This would suggest his final resting position once he was placed in the bin."

"So he ended up head first and resting to his right, from what you're suggesting?"

"Correct. He also has discolouration through extensive bruising around the abdomen and chest."

"From being hit or punched?"

"No. That type of bruising would be smaller and more random in appearance. This bruising covers flatter, broad areas of his chest and abdomen. I'll look at it a bit closer to check for internal trauma, but my guess would be that the bruising is consistent with being picked up in a bear hug type of hold." Cara demonstrated by outstretching her arms and gripping her left wrist with her right hand. "Extreme pressure would cause that type of bruising to the skin of the abdomen and pronounced areas where the skin is stretched tight, for example, across the ribcage."

Scott stood with his arms crossed. He nodded as a mental picture formed in his mind of how the victim had been disposed of. Frankly, any mental picture he could conjure up would be better than seeing a corpse with its ribcage opened, the top of its skull and brain missing, and the pathologist enjoying every minute. He thought of Cara Hall as being some prospective gold miner excited about discovering a vein of gold ore in a rock face.

"Can you tell me anything about the knife wound?" Scott was keen to hurry up and leave Cara to her examination. The longer he stood there, the more he was forced to take in the smell – and the more objections his stomach made. He noticed the odd bluebottle looping around in the space above them.

This place is so gross.

"Yes, I can. This is a fascinating case, Inspector."

"Fascinating. Really?"

Cara became animated in her explanation. "The wound doesn't resemble what you'd normally associate with a stabbing. Often, the weapon of choice is something like a lock knife, sheath knife or kitchen knife, which has a short, thin, stiff blade about seven centimetres long. Those give clean-cut edges, but a kitchen knife tends to bend and can break easily with minimum force, especially if the tip hits bone and becomes embedded in it."

Scott raised a brow. This was starting to get interesting.

"This knife was a lot bigger and longer because the entry point is here." Cara placed a hand either side of the victim's head and turned it forty-five degrees to the right to show the left side of his neck. "Then what's more unusual is that there's an exit point here." She pointed to an open wound just above the right clavicle.

"That's a heavy stab wound, then?" Scott asked.

"It is, and what becomes apparent now that I've opened up the area is the internal damage." Cara grabbed some forceps to pull the neck area apart and expose the internal structures, intended to give Scott a better view.

She pointed at an area. "If you look through the magnifying lamp now, can you see the torn edges of the wound?"

Scott peered through a large, six-inch magnifying glass that had a ring of brightness illuminating the outer edge. He saw the area and nodded.

"A normal knife wouldn't cause such rough edges," she said. "This is the type of stab wound a survival knife causes. They create different wound impressions because of the serrations on the non-cutting edge, which act like a saw. This is what has torn the edge and not given it a clean incision. You can also see... the knife tore through the carotid artery, causing a massive haemorrhage, and also took out the trachea too."

"How big is one of these survival knives?" Scott asked.

"They vary but are normally six to eight inches long. Some are longer, and I'm talking about blade length here, Inspector, not including the handle. I'll be able to give you a better indication later when I get stuck in, if you pardon the pun." She smiled.

"So that could explain why there's an exit point?"

"Most certainly. Extreme force was used, and from the angle of the entry and exit points, a downward action was applied, which offers far more force than, shall we say, an underarm thrust or prodding action. There's what we call hilt bruising, too, where the knife has been driven in with such force that it's gone up into the hilt guard. Where the guard impacted the skin has caused distinctive bruising at one edge of the wound.

"It will all be in my report, Inspector, but I'd say that the assailant chose their type of weapon carefully. They knew they could target the great vessels of the neck. Provided they applied enough force, they could *drop* the victim straight away with consciousness lost soon after. Death came almost immediately. This chap bled to death in a matter of moments."

"Thanks, Dr Hall. That gives me a lot to go on. I'm going to head back to update the DCI and team, and I'll wait for your report. Thanks for rushing this through so quickly. I owe you one." Scott turned and walked away.

"Inspector?" Cara called out.

Scott stopped mid-step and turned back. "Yes?"

With a look of concern on her face, the pathologist said, "This was no ordinary knife attack. The knife and victim were chosen for a reason."

Her parting comment sent a chill through Scott's body. It was what he already suspected.

9

It was late afternoon before Scott returned to the station in John Street. Brighton police station was an imposing five-storey building in an elevated position, neatly tucked away behind Victoria Gardens and the university's Grand Parade campus. At this time of year, the sun was low in the sky, its heat output modest; the nights drew in early and the temperature dropped quickly.

Scott rubbed his hands together and blew air into them to warm them up. He looked up at the darkening clear sky.

It's going to be a chilly one again tonight.

He nodded at the desk sergeant as he headed indoors.

CID was located on the first floor, but space was at a premium with a desk-hopping policy in place. Since the budget cuts had drastically slimmed down the team size, all remaining officers currently had their own workstations. However, this arrangement was a temporary one. Once the multimillion-pound refurbishment programme was completed, hot-desking would become a formal requirement.

The team briefing, to be headed up by him, had been scheduled by the DCI, Scott's superior. Scott would have preferred to start earlier, but the DCI had stipulated a time that suited her.

It was scheduled for six p.m., which gave Scott ten minutes to grab a coffee from the vending machine. What came out didn't look like and often didn't taste like coffee. It was a lottery as to what he might get. Holding the Styrofoam cup in one hand, whilst carrying a folder, notebook and mobile phone in his other, Scott walked into the briefing room on the top floor of the station, where the team was already gathering.

Moments later, Detective Chief Inspector Jane Harvey entered, causing the conversation between Mike and Raj to dissipate into nothing more than background murmurs.

The contrast in look between Scott and his superior couldn't have been more different.

Scott stood at six feet, with short, dark brown hair finger-combed to look fashionably unkempt. He had an athletic build from all his years of cycling, gruelling gym sessions and his most recent fitness craze of TRX sessions. A lover of style and fashion, he took pride in his appearance, choosing the most fashionable labels. His favourite suits were all by Paul Smith, finished off with Church's brogues. His dress sense and handsome looks had prompted many discussions amongst female colleagues at the station.

The DCI, on the other hand, always looked as if she'd dressed blindly in the dark with her floral tops and thigh-length Aztec-print cardigans. Along with her halo of plump grey curls, her five-foot short stature, wide girth and crazy stare, she was often described by station colleagues as cantankerous, argumentative and obstinate. She was what they called an old-school copper. At fifty-five, she had stayed on long past the thirty years' service and had chosen to delay her retirement.

DCI Harvey was more interested in results than paperwork, bureaucracy and performance targets, which brought her into direct conflict with her superiors and the ethos of modern-day policing. There were rumours that she'd outstayed her usefulness, and that senior management wanted her replaced with a dynamic *yes* person.

She was anything but a yes person.

Despite her eccentricities, DCI Harvey never hesitated to support and stand by her officers, a quality greatly appreciated by all members of the team.

She took her seat at the back of the room, a favourite place for her to observe her team without being a distraction.

Scott looked up to see Abby walk in. She joined Mike, Raj and Sian, who were already seated at or perched on the table.

Scott took his place at the front of the room beside the whiteboard. He placed a picture of Edward Stone on it.

"Okay, team, as you are aware, we had a fatality this morning. Mike, can you tell us what you know?"

Mike stood up. "Okay, guv. The victim is Edward Stone, aged thirty-four. He's the owner of two nightclubs: the Phoenix in Preston Street and Urban on the seafront. He's known to us and has convictions for assault and fraud. The assault was on another clubber when Stone was twenty-seven. The fraud was a stolen chequebook scam. He lives, or should I say, lived in Fourth Avenue, Hove, with his fiancée, Vicky Bright."

"Okay, thanks, Mike." Scott checked his notepad before continuing, "The PM was conducted this afternoon, and we'll get the full report shortly. What I want to bring to your attention is the method used. The assailant used a survival knife, probably with a large blade, around six to eight inches long. It's not the usual weapon of choice when it comes to stabbings."

He noted the looks of concern and curiosity amongst the officers gathered as they exchanged glances.

"Any idea as to why a survival knife was used? I mean, they're big enough buggers to kill a large bloody animal," asked Raj. He used his hands to emphasise the length of the blade.

"That's the concern here, Raj. The path, Cara Hall, said that this type of knife was chosen for a reason, to cause maximum damage and, as she put it, 'to drop the victim'."

"So it was planned, guv?" asked Sian, the newest member of the team, having joined only six months earlier.

"Too complicated to be a random attack," replied Scott. "It wasn't robbery, as no personal items appear to have been taken. Having seen the injuries up close, it was premeditated. The killer took out the carotid artery and trachea. The victim not only bled to death but was starved of oxygen." He added more, "There's another unusual aspect to the killing. The victim had three twenty-pound notes stuffed in his mouth. I don't know the meaning yet, so I'm open to suggestions."

"Perhaps he didn't like hiding his cash under the mattress," quipped Mike. The suggestion was met with low laughter and groans.

"Highly unlikely, but thanks for that intelligent guess, Mike." Scott's response received a round of laughter and ribbing.

"Everyone, please." Scott brought order to the room. "We need to start focusing on Stone's background first thing tomorrow. I know Sunday is a rest day for a few of us, but time is of the essence, so we need to get a move on pretty sharpish." He looked to his DC. "Abby and I will visit his clubs. Mike, I want you to organise a search of his apartment. Take Raj with you. We need to look for paperwork, mobile phones, laptops and anything else that may be of interest." He looked at his superior. "Ma'am, can we get a few uniforms to help out tomorrow?"

DCI Harvey nodded. "Leave it with me, Scott."

"Sian?" Scott said.

She looked up from making notes. "Yes, guv?"

"I want you to do some door-to-door work, see what other traders knew about Stone, if they saw anything unusual during the last twenty-four hours. And check with control, see if we've got any CCTV footage." Scott looked to the back of the room. "Anything you'd like to add, ma'am?"

DCI Harvey sat quietly, arms crossed, no expression. "Nope, nothing further to add. I just need you to hold back a few moments after the briefing, DI Baker, so we can talk to the press liaison and agree on a suitable press release."

Scott rubbed his tired eyes and blew out a breath.

"Okay, team, let's get to work on this first thing tomorrow. Head home and get some rest. It's going to be a busy day."

10

Sleep eluded Scott that night. He tossed and turned, occasionally drifting off just to jerk awake a short time later. Each time he drifted off, that dark memory crept up on him again.

He was running... running helplessly across the road. He didn't want to go back and see the aftermath, but he had to. He knew fear and utter confusion would engulf him.

He looked over his shoulder and saw a dark, swirling mass scudding across the ground and headed in his direction. He screamed and tried to run faster, but the ground under his feet slowed him down. With each step, his feet grew heavier, and he fought to drag himself free.

The dark cloud closed in, shadows churning around him. The blackness threatened to consume him. The opaque abyss swallowed him, and an icy chill instantly wrapped around his body. He reached one arm out, reaching desperately for someone, anyone, to grab him and pull him out of this quagmire. His quivering voice cried out for help. His fingertips were all that remained visible, and they threatened to disappear into the murk of obscurity.

Moments before vanishing into the vortex, Scott jolted awake.

His breath came out in ragged gasps. Tears slid down his cheeks, making his pillow damp. The bedding was a jumbled heap by his feet.

He lay there for a few minutes trying to calm down. He hated his nightmares. Not only did they deprive him of sleep, but they dragged him to a place that he had consciously tried to bury. Desperate to shake off this melancholy mood, he climbed out of bed and peered out through his blinds.

The night sky was brightening, giving it a predawn lightness. As hard as he tried, he couldn't stop thinking about the nightmare. He'd had it before, and it always left him drained and aching with loneliness. He missed Tina and Becky so much, the light and love from his life. Both had been extinguished in a blink of the eye, and he'd been powerless to do anything about it. There were many times he wished that he'd joined them.

After chasing away those troubling thoughts, his mind turned to another disturbing subject: the callous murder of Edward Stone.

Scott needed to get out and clear his head. It was approaching six a.m., and the light was breaking over Hove. He threw on a pair of joggers and a hoodie and headed out for a quick walk to grab some fresh morning air and shake off his dark mood.

Within ten minutes he was out on the Kingsway, where he cut through the Hove and Kingsway Bowls and Social Club lawns and small, green-roofed beach huts that skirted the pebble beach.

Standing on the beach in the crispness of the cold spring

morning, Scott closed his eyes and took lungfuls of fresh sea air.

There was something magical and soothing about sea air and its ability to calm and centre him. This fresh natural force coursed through every muscle, vein and cell of his being, ridding him of the sickening dull feeling that resided in the pit of his stomach and the middle of his heart.

Scott opened his eyes at the sound of gulls and their distinctive chatter. At that moment, with the chorus of seagulls overhead and the waves gently lapping onto the pebbles, Scott couldn't think of anywhere else he'd rather be.

This was his own little piece of paradise, his way of escaping reality and the parts of life most people never saw. A place that offered a temporary calmness from the pain and dark nightmares that haunted him when he closed his eyes at night.

11

It was just after nine a.m. when Scott arrived outside the Phoenix nightclub in Preston Street.

Less than twenty-four hours ago the street had been the scene of a horrific murder, and for the best part of the day, the street had been sealed off whilst scientific services officers bagged and catalogued every scrap of evidence. The area had been photographed in meticulous detail. Any relevant signs or points of interest like bloodstains were marked, numbered and photographed.

With the advent of body cams a few years ago and, more recently, police-issued mobile phones with FaceTime capability, officers on the ground could relay a crime scene back to officers at the station for immediate assessment and input. Scott found these real-time photos and videos were invaluable to officers who were unable to attend the scene, helping them get a faster understanding.

The scene had been a calm but busy hub yesterday as the area was marked out and searched in a linear pattern. An orderly line of officers inched forward to ensure nothing was overlooked.

Now the street was open for business once again. The blood had been washed away by council workers, traders were going about their business, and curious members of the public were turning up in the hope of seeing some grisly remnants of the aftermath.

"Today's news is tomorrow's chip wrapper," Scott reminded himself.

He looked up at the Phoenix nightclub. Both it and the Urban had been kept under police guard since yesterday's events, to stop anyone from going in and potentially tampering with evidence, or disturbing clues to the deceased's last few hours. As Scott approached the main entrance, he was met by a uniformed officer who acknowledged his arrival.

"Morning, Constable. Anything to report?" Scott asked.

"No, sir. Nothing more than curious onlookers asking a few questions," replied PC Oju. He was almost as tall as Scott, but more slender, with dark Afro-Caribbean features that offset his bright smile.

As Scott waited for Abby to arrive, his phone sprang into life and vibrated against his chest, heralding the arrival of an email. Scott reached in to grab it from his inside jacket pocket and then proceeded to unlock the phone using the elaborate security swipe pattern he'd created.

"For fuck's sake," he muttered. On the third attempt, he finally unlocked the phone and made a mental note to find an easier way to lock it.

The email was from Crime Scene Manager Matt Allan.

Hi Scott,

My team is still poring over the evidence collected. However, we found prints on the bloodstained twenty-pound notes, and these will be analysed and cross-refer-

enced later today. We also sent the victim's mobile phone on to the high-tech unit for analysis. All results will be with you in the next 24-48 hours.

Speak soon,
Matt.

Scott felt encouraged by the news, but nevertheless cautious. He knew that the identification of prints could lead to nothing, but there was always hope of an early breakthrough either with a print match or from phone records.

As he looked down the street to the seafront, he saw Abby finishing her discussion with Sian before leaving her to carry out further door-to-door enquiries with residents and traders.

Abby joined him, and they headed into the club.

Scott was greeted by the smell of stale beer and mustiness from the lack of ventilation and natural light. The club itself was a well-proportioned space. Even still, Abby commented that her living room floor had more space than the dance-floor area she stood on.

"What happened to the days of a nightclub looking like a proper club, with a big dance floor?" Abby said with amusement.

The club reminded Scott of an informal airport first-class lounge – it was wide but not very deep. To the left was a bar with the usual spread of alcoholic bottles in front of a mirrored wall. The bar itself was an all glass and mirror affair. The bar area was illuminated by gaudy purple and blue neon lights.

In the middle was a small, black marble dance floor, which must have seen very little action judging by how shiny and clean it looked.

To the right, and taking up at least two-thirds of the nightclub, were eight sets of purple sofas set around small white, round tables. Each table and sofa had embedded lights in them, which gave out a soft, white glow.

As Scott looked around, there was nothing to suggest that the events of the night would end the way they did. Everything appeared to be where it should have been; nothing was broken or damaged; there was no evidence of an altercation within the club that could have carried on outside.

"There are enough bulbs here to bring down the local power grid!" Abby said as she looked up and spotted the gantry of powerful lights aimed towards the dance floor.

"I know, can you imagine the electricity bill?" Scott replied with a laugh and a dismissive shake of his head.

Scott recalled his university days, heading off to the Escape and other Gloucester nightclubs where he spent the best part of the night bumping into other revellers, a problem that often worsened as the night wore on. A combination of no air conditioning, overcrowding, cheap drinks and condensation dripping off the ceilings all added to the underground feel. Not like this place.

The good old days. He smiled at the memory.

"I never saw a club like this in my day."

"Nor mine," said Abby in agreement.

They walked on to the back of the club and Stone's office, passing by the tacky high-class decor the club was attempting to portray. Inside his office was plush, navy carpets, ornate tall plants and a bank of monitors. A dark mahogany desk and a leather chair took centre stage in the room.

Scott and Abby wandered off in different directions as they looked through the desk drawers and the various assortment of paperwork left behind.

Their search of Stone's desk threw up nothing of importance, but the laptop, files and folders would be bagged up and recorded for review back at the station. As they moved their attention away from his desk, Abby found a safe buried in the wall, hidden behind some garish wall art.

"Guv, there's a safe here, but it's locked. We need to get this opened."

"Get on to control and ask them to arrange for a locksmith to attend. We need to see if there's anything inside of interest."

With that, Abby left the room to make the call outside.

As Scott moved around the office, his attention turned back to the corner of the room behind the door, where there was a squat, dusty mirrored table set between two low armchairs. Moving towards the table for a closer look, he noticed that the dust wasn't the type that had collected through a lack of cleaning. He could see a light scattering of white granular powder.

If his hunch was right, then these were the remains of a class A substance.

12

Abby was just coming off her call when Scott approached her. He tapped her on the arm to get her attention.

"Yes, guv?"

"Organise a dog. We've got evidence of class A activity on the small table in the office. Meet me outside when you're done."

Phone reception must have been intermittent in the club, because no sooner had Scott stepped outside on to the pavement, his phone buzzed in his pocket. He checked it and saw he had missed a call and text message from Raj.

Scott hit the redial, and on the third ring Raj answered.

"Guv, we've searched Stone's flat and found a black holdall at the bottom of a wardrobe in the third bedroom. There were a few large packets of white powder we believe to be class A. We've bagged it up and will bring it in. His missus swears blind that she knew nothing about it."

"Do you believe her?"

"Hard to say, guv. She looked mortified, but she could be putting it on."

"Okay, Raj, good work. Let's get it tested, and once we have confirmation, we can pull her in for further questioning if needed."

Abby joined him outside, and Scott relayed the news to her as they walked to Stone's second club called Urban, on the seafront.

Urban didn't throw up anything that raised suspicion. All paperwork on the desk had been bagged up and logged in the same way as at the Phoenix. They did, however, notice a strong smell of cannabis in the toilets, and Scott instructed Abby to get the drugs dog to check both clubs.

HIS STOMACH RUMBLED, and Scott suggested that he and Abby grab an early lunch while the canine unit was working. They headed off to one of Scott's favourites: all'Angelo in East Street.

Scott settled for a tuna melt panini, whilst Abby picked at her spicy halloumi and roasted vegetable salad.

"You going to have time to head off to the gym later today?" he asked her.

"Depends how we get on today, guv. I've not had a moment to myself for a few days, as I had the kids this weekend. If I can't today, then I'll go tomorrow morning and do a couple of classes before my shift starts at two."

Scott smiled and shook his head. He used his napkin to wipe his mouth. "Flipping hell, I just don't know where you get the energy. One class is enough, but you do two or three classes in a row. You're either a machine or have a screw loose," he replied in bewilderment.

"Oi, watch it." She laughed. "No, it's fine. You wouldn't make it through circuits, you lightweight."

"Excuse me, you'll find that I can give you a run for your money."

"Dream on." Abby laughed again, this time tossing her head back in an exaggerated movement.

She continued, more serious, "Exercise is my release. You know how tough our job can be. Look at last week, when we got called in to go after that armed burglar with the TDA. I came on shift at two p.m. on Tuesday and finished at one p.m. Wednesday because we needed to find him, get him charged, off the streets and the file to CPS within twenty-four hours. I was shattered, and it took me two days to get my body clock back in line." She sighed. "Going to the gym helps my mind to relax. I must admit though, it's a tough call. Sometimes I want to go to the gym; other times I just want to be at home with the kids. I don't see them enough as it is, and I hate having to palm them off on friends and grandparents as it is."

Scott shrugged. "Fair point."

"As much as I love the job, guv, it does get me down sometimes. Routine goes out the window, the hours are unpredictable, and life can get lonely. Look at how many relationships fall apart in the force; it's the same with all the emergency services."

For a moment Scott was drawn into his darkest memories as he thought about his own family.

Abby continued, "Look at me, single mum, two kids I hardly see, no time for a relationship, and each month I go overdrawn on my cards. I'm hardly a good advert for the force."

Even though Abby was talking about the daily struggle to balance life, Scott would have given anything to have that dilemma in his life right now.

13

The target had parked in the residents' parking bays after one of his clandestine meetings. The area was poorly lit with one solitary street light casting dim shadows. It was two thirty a.m., meaning residents of this council estate would be in bed. No one would be around to disturb this moment of revenge.

He is evil – he needs to be dealt with.

The killer had watched from a spot in the shadows on this chilly spring night. The only clue to give him away was his icy breath that was quiet – unnaturally quiet. Not many chose to walk these streets at night, as they feared the marauding groups of teenagers hell-bent on terrorising the neighbourhood.

Though the area was known to the police for its vandalism, drug dealing and the permanent smell of marijuana that hung in the air, a police officer walking the beat was unheard of.

Drug dens were tucked away from prying eyes. Children on bikes were employed by dealers to peddle their valuable merchandise. Using children as their drug mules lessened their risks – and their overheads. It was just business to them. They weren't worried or concerned about the misery it caused, or the suffering it brought to the vulnerable, or the dependencies it created, or the crime needed to fuel insatiable habits.

The target opened the boot to his Mercedes E220, unaware of the approaching threat.

The killer came up to him from behind. He was braver this time, new bravado swelling inside him. He wasn't scared; he was determined to stick to his plan and do the right thing.

He held the gleaming blade high above his head as he closed in. The victim had little time to react before he looped an arm around the man's head to trap him before plunging the tip of the blade deep into his victim's neck.

The victim reared up, but his strength drained away fast as the blade plunged deeper. The man fell forward into the open boot of his car, his left hand coming up to the wound. The killer withdrew the blade before plunging it in again, impaling the victim's hand in the process and pinning it to his neck.

The victim didn't move after that. He lay there head first slumped in the boot. The only sound was the gurgling of blood as it escaped with the man's final breaths.

The killer, still hell-bent on meting out his own justice, twisted the blade left and right. The victim's mutilated hand twisted and turned with the knife; the sound of wet flesh tearing reached him as the blade mangled the flesh.

The job was done. Sinews of flesh and veins clung to the blade, a testament to the ferocity of his assault.

Using one hand, the killer pulled back the victim's head by his hair, then shoved something into the gaping mouth that was frozen in silent horror at what had taken place just moments ago. He dropped the man's head.

As the killer stood there breathing rapidly, sweat beading

on his forehead and creeping down the centre of his spine, he felt cold and numb. It wasn't the cold night air that made him feel that way; it was the lack of feeling and emotion created by the dark void inside him.

He turned and walked away, his trousers damp once again.

14

The morning brought a fresh set of tasks for the team. A press release in the *Argus* and *Brighton & Hove Independent* the day before had led to a growing list of messages.

There were a few calls from members of the public regarding miscellaneous issues. However, many called in to air their gripes about crime in the town and the lack of police action.

As Scott knew, all the information gathered had to be reviewed and either followed up or dismissed as inconsequential. Any leads at this stage could offer an insight that Scott and the team needed.

As his officers Raj and Sian sifted through the messages, Scott got down to checking on the other ongoing eleven case files from his team that needed a weekly review.

With cases that included two reported rapes, one attempted rape, a death from a suspicious house fire, a person falling from the multistorey car park in Worthing, and numerous burglaries, his team were stretched to breaking point.

But based on the likelihood of a successful conclusion and the severity of the cases, a big case like a murder meant he would need to prioritise resources. Supervising his officers, case file reviews and endless reporting to senior management left Scott feeling frustrated, stressed and like he was always chasing his tail.

THE BRIEFING ROOM was large enough to accommodate an oval table with sixteen chairs around it. There was a large whiteboard on one wall and a sixty-inch TV at one end of the room.

From this floor, there was a good view across the city centre on a clear day, but today, the clouds cast a heavy, grey canopy across the city that created dampness in the air.

Scott addressed his team. "Guys, I know you're all tired, and you've been working flat out, so let's get this briefing wrapped up and crack on. Sian, do you want to kick off first?"

Sian was still relatively new to her role and team. An officer for five years, making the switch over to CID had always been her ambition. She was of average build, not thin or overweight and dressed conservatively, opting for A-line skirts, Next blouses, and low-heel court shoes. She wore her dark brown hair in a high ponytail. The look was finished off with black-rimmed glasses.

Sian was ambitious, diligent and hard-working. Still only twenty-seven, she'd never hidden the fact that she wanted to succeed in her career, and sought promotion. In Scott's development reviews with her, he'd been impressed with her grasp of PACE, the Police and Criminal Evidence Act, the code of ethics by which the police structured their work. He'd mused that she must have swallowed the manuals whole.

"Nothing to report," Sian said. "The crew at the China

Garden, near where the body was found, tipped out about twelve thirty a.m., and they saw nothing. No one at the hotel on the corner had anything new to share. The casino near the club drew a blank too. We also checked with the residents of the apartments above the Chinese, but other than some residents complaining to us about the smell of fried food from downstairs... like we're going to do anything about it," she said with a shrug. "There was nothing, guv."

"So, nothing then." Scott sighed. "Thought that might be a long shot. CCTV, Sian?"

"Nope, nothing there either, guv. Nearest camera is at the top of Preston Street on Western Road, and it was pointing along Western Road at the time, I'm afraid."

"Sly. Our killer is smart as well as dangerous, or just plain lucky." Scott exhaled as he locked his hands on top of his head. "Mike?"

Mike was in the middle of emptying a can of Red Bull. He looked up, startled. A dribble of the drink ran down his chin, much to Raj's amusement, who was perched on the edge of a chair beside him.

"Get this man a bib, someone," Raj teased. Mike glared at him, embarrassed, whilst giving him the middle finger.

"Forensics have come back to confirm that the bags of powder from Stone's flat and the club were cocaine. There were cocaine traces on the table in Stone's office and interestingly on many of the tables in the club. There were traces of coke and marijuana in the toilets of Urban." Mike sighed in frustration. "There are no matching prints on the system for those found on the twenty-pound notes, guv."

"It looks like they turned a blind eye to drugs in the clubs, and Stone must have known about it or, at worst, was supplying it," Scott said. He closed his eyes and massaged the back of his neck.

"Could give us a motive," piped up Sian.

"That's certainly a possibility." Scott opened his eyes. "Sian, I want you to get on to the high-tech unit and see if they've got everything off his phone yet. Also contact his phone provider for phone records. Any problems with a lack of cooperation, let me know."

"Will do, guv."

"Abby, tomorrow I want you to start checking out the drugs angle. Tug the collars of the dealers and the users to see if anyone knows about the drugs scene at the Phoenix and Urban."

Abby nodded.

"Anything else worth raising?" asked Scott, looking around those gathered.

A knock on the door interrupted the meeting. Seeing the desk sergeant through the glass panels, Scott waved him in.

"Sorry to interrupt, sir, but I thought you should know that a body's just been found by uniformed officers. The victim's been stabbed through the neck."

15

By the time Scott and Abby arrived at the second crime scene, the circus was in full swing. There was a hive of activity behind the blue and white tape cordon set up around the residents' car parking in Warbleton Close, on the White Hawk estate.

It was an estate well known to the police. Due to a lack of investment in local services, broken promises from successive governments and high unemployment amongst the locals, the estate had its fair share of bad press.

If you asked most of the residents about the area, they'd have plenty to say about how good it was living in a close-knit community. However, antisocial behaviour, criminal damage and violent and sexual crimes had tarnished the estate in the eyes of external observers and gave the local tabloids plenty to write about.

Scott had parked on the corner of Whitehawk Crescent behind a squad car. A growing crowd of locals hovered, perversely curious to see what had happened during the night. After being let through the cordon by a police constable, Scott and Abby walked towards the area where the body had been found.

The residents' parking was set off the street on the right-hand side, about twenty yards up the street. It was a small car park that allowed residents to park up to eight cars. It was enclosed on three sides by houses and garden walls. A white tent had been erected over the crime scene to preserve the area and to stop the curtain twitchers from getting a good eyeful.

Scott and Abby donned their protective suits, gloves and masks before going any farther. The crime scene investigators were examining the area, taking photos and documenting the evidence. There were two other cars in the car park, which were also being examined.

To the left of the car park Scott saw Crime Scene Manager Matt Allan sitting in his car with the door open, engrossed in a conversation on his mobile. Scott and Abby approached the white tent and were just about to open the flap when another SOCO stepped out.

"I hope you weren't expecting to go inside. We haven't finished yet," she said in a dismissive voice that implied they were in the way.

Scott bit his bottom lip. Abby glanced at him. She knew him well enough to know he was trying to keep a lid on the expletives that were threatening to explode from his mouth.

He replied with a hint of sarcasm in his tone. "Of course, we don't want to get in your way, wouldn't want to disturb you doing your job."

The SOCO's eyes widened, and Scott could tell she was riled.

He continued, softening his tone, "Look, I haven't got all day to wait around. I just want to peek in through the flap so I know what we're dealing with."

The SOCO didn't reply but gave a cursory flick of her head to confirm permission to peek inside the tent.

Scott exhaled deeply. *Cheeky fucker.*

As he and Abby peeked in through the flap, they were confronted with the lower half of a man's body half in half out of the boot space of a Mercedes. Within the tent, SOCO had set up arc lights to illuminate the scene. With it being early spring, natural light was still too dull and flat.

From this angle, it was hard to see the victim's upper torso and the injuries. But with Captain von SOCO barking orders behind them about what they could and couldn't do, both officers retreated for the time being.

"Abby, can you run the plates through the system to see if we can get an ID? And I'll have a word with Matt."

"Will do, guv."

16

Scott hung by Matt's van door as he finished up his call.

"Morning, Matt. Have you got anything for us yet?"

The lead SOCO shook his head. "No chance, buddy. We've only been on the scene for under an hour, so we're just midway through the analysis."

Scott nodded. He rested one elbow on the roof of the white van as he glanced around and took in the neighbourhood. He noticed a distinct lack of character about the place. All the houses bore an identical resemblance, constructed in a methodical and economical way with small gardens surrounded by waist-high brick walls.

Matt continued, "We'll be finishing up with the victim shortly. We just need to go over the surrounding area first. However, initial inspections suggest a forceful impact to the side of the neck. That's all for the moment, mate."

"Okay. Keep me informed."

As Scott was about to walk away, Matt added, "It looks like a similar attack to the one we've just had. Lone male, trauma to the neck, attacked at night. Hard to believe it's a coincidence." His voice trailed off as he zoned off into the distance.

"That's what concerns me," Scott replied. "Thanks."

As Scott headed back to Abby, pathologist Cara Hall had just arrived and was making a beeline for the tent.

"Dr Hall," he called out.

Cara turned to greet him with a smile. She held a hand up to stop him. "Before you start, don't crowd me, don't press me, don't annoy me and don't on any account mess up my crime scene. Now, how can I help?"

"Straight to the point as usual, Dr Hall." Scott smiled. "I'll leave you in peace to do what you need to do. If you're able, can you give me a cause of death so I have something to go on until you've completed your PM?" Scott asked.

"I'll try my best," she said and continued to the tent.

Abby was about to fill in Scott on her findings when Mike and Raj arrived.

The four of them convened a safe distance from the tent near the cordon, and she continued with what she'd discovered through the police databases.

"Guv, the car is registered to a Dave Fraser, thirty-nine, and he's known to us." Mike and Scott shot each other a glance.

"We've nicked him a few times," said Mike.

Abby continued, "He's got a charge sheet as long as your arm, a major known supplier around town."

Scott didn't like the sound of this but nodded. The first murder was proving a challenge, but to be faced with two similar attacks in just three days worried him. He knew DCI Harvey would be banging on his door for answers, and as it stood, he didn't have much to go on except two dead men with previous convictions, both killed in a similar manner in under a week.

"Okay, well, let's get him formally ID'd. Hopefully SOCO can get us his personal possessions shortly, and we can go from there."

Scott instructed Mike and Raj to start following up on the door-to-door enquiries that uniform had already started. "It's a built-up area, but well shielded. The car park has a bit of light from that street light, so someone might have seen something suspicious or out of the ordinary in the last twenty-four hours."

Scott knew he was clutching at straws; relations between the police and locals were strained at the best of times. Residents would rather turn a blind eye than be seen helping the police.

17

Mr Albert Norris, a local resident, had made the initial call reporting the murder. Scott headed over to his house, which was across the road from the scene.

It was the end house of a terrace with three identical properties. They were all brown brick-built, with low-rise roofs and exposed brick porches.

Scott found it odd that this particular property had a front door and a small window to the right and a first-floor window directly above the door, but the property seemed to be missing a large ground-floor lounge window and a first-floor bedroom window. It appeared as if the builders had forgotten to leave spaces for the windows and just carried on building the rest of the house.

Scott rang the doorbell, and a uniformed officer answered moments later, clutching a mug of tea.

Scott presented his warrant card to the officer, who acknowledged it with, "Morning, sir. Mr Norris is in the kitchen."

The house was dark inside with dull ceilings and tobacco-stained walls that left a golden honey shade. He walked along the hallway that split the property in half.

To his right was the downstairs cloakroom with stairs leading to the first floor. To the left a lounge with a blue-velour sofa suite that had seen better days, and a small TV sitting on a stand.

The kitchen at the end of the hallway was small and cramped. Most of the work surfaces were covered in a mixture of unopened post and flyers and a few empty plates with remnants of dried food on them.

Mr Norris sat at a small square dining table that had two wooden chairs opposite each other. He was a small gentleman, thinly built, his face framed with metal-rimmed glasses. His grey hair had been oiled down with a left-hand parting the way you'd expect your granddad to have. He wore the grey classic polyester trousers that so many of his generation wore, with a white shirt, tie and black tank top jumper.

Scott held a degree of respect for this generation; they grew up with manners, and were always dressed sensibly, even if the look wasn't to his taste.

Mr Norris was holding a cup of tea between both hands when he looked up to see Scott peer in through the kitchen door.

Scott pulled out his warrant card. "Mr Norris, I'm Detective Inspector Scott Baker from Brighton CID. I understand you made the initial call this morning. May I ask you a few questions?"

"Of course," he replied. "Can I offer you some tea or coffee?"

Scott declined his offer.

"Can you tell me what happened?"

"Well, I'm not sure I can be of much help, as I told the officers."

"I can assure you, Mr Norris, anything you mention could

be vital in our investigations and help us to piece together what happened."

Norris nodded. "Okay, well, I got up about two fifteen a.m. because I needed a piss. The old bladder ain't what it used to be, if you know what I mean."

Scott nodded, not wishing to interrupt him.

"Anyway, as I was coming out of the bathroom, I thought I heard a bit of shuffling out front. I just thought it was cats or foxes sniffing around the bins across the road. I went to the front window and didn't see much other than someone walking away from the car park."

"What time would that have been?" Scott asked as he leant forward with interest. He was excited; this was the first possible breakthrough in this series of killings.

It took Mr Norris a few moments to answer Scott's question. He had digressed to recall how serving in the war meant he was up all hours and had never really settled back into a decent bedtime routine since then. With his wife, Edith, passing away some years back, he struggled to sleep at night.

"Perhaps it's the loneliness." Norris trailed off, looking into the bottom of his cup.

"Mr Norris?" Scott jolted him back to the present, even though he didn't want to interrupt him.

"Sorry, Detective Inspector... Hmm, it was probably around two-thirty-ish, I'd imagine," he said, holding his chin high.

"And what did you see? Can you describe the person? Male, female? Tall, short? Wearing any clothing that stands out? Anything like that would be of great help."

"My eyesight ain't what it used to be, and I didn't have my glasses on. All I can say is the person was wearing dark clothes..." He paused to look up towards the ceiling, as if checking his recollection. "Black probably... definitely dark... they had their hands in their pockets and a hood pulled up over their head. I couldn't honestly say if they were male or female. Anyway, that's hard to tell sometimes in daylight, don't you think – with the way they dress?" He waved a hand near his ear. "Blokes wearing earrings, women wearing torn jeans and spitting... What's next, hey? There's no respect these days... Bring back national service, I say." He concluded with a firm nod and a light thump of his clenched hand on the table.

Scott hoped the old fella felt better for getting that off his chest.

"Where was this person when you saw them?" Scott asked.

"They were walking out of the car park and heading down the road to Whitehawk Crescent."

"Mr Norris, you've been very helpful. Thank you for your time. And I'll arrange for one of my officers to get a full statement from you today." Scott pulled a business card out from his wallet. "Don't hesitate to call me if you think of anything else."

18

Mr Norris mumbled in the background, keen to carry on the conversation, as he followed Scott to the door. Scott smiled and pulled himself away as politely as he could without hurting the old man's feelings before heading back to the car park.

Cara was putting away the last of her things into her car. She looked up as Scott approached and greeted him with a smile.

"Safe to come near you?" Scott questioned her.

She tipped her head to one side. "Is that the best you can do? We've got to stop meeting like this." She looked around in mock fear, her eyes wide. "The neighbours will talk."

"I think that's the least of their worries, don't you? I've got an old fella who's an eyewitness but couldn't see much because he didn't have his glasses on, and we've already had many of his neighbours expressing their concerns about their own safety. I'm having to draft in a load of PCSOs to go from door to door to reassure residents that this was an isolated incident and that we'll be increasing our patrols in the area for the next few days."

"You have to feel for them though," she said, looking past Scott to the row of houses on the opposite side of the street. Residents gathered in small huddles, concern and worry etched on their faces. She tilted her head to one side and pursed her lips in sympathy. "Many are quite elderly so naturally feel more vulnerable."

Scott glanced over his shoulder to see what Cara was looking at.

She continued, "Think about how you would feel if you were their age and a man had been violently stabbed to death just yards from your front door. You'd be terrified to leave your house. I bet you if you went over and ask them that very same question, you'd get the same response."

Scott smiled. Everything that Cara was saying was true, but with the frenetic pace of any investigation, he never had time to truly reflect on the impact that a murder could have on local residents and the wider community. To him it was another statistic, another investigation, and another suspect to identify, track down and bring to justice. He didn't have time to reflect on the emotional impact, and the concerns and fears that it raised amongst ordinary members of the public.

"So what have we got?" he asked, keen to keep on topic.

"Similar to the last killing, I'm afraid. Stab wound to the neck; bit messier this one though. The weapon used must have been pretty big to create such localised trauma. I think the person you're dealing with is incredibly dangerous and volatile. It was a ferocious attack." Cara paused for a moment. "Someone likes giving their money away."

"Sorry?" Scott asked.

Cara looked up from checking her messages on her phone. "The three twenty-pound notes stuffed in the vic's mouth."

"Are we dealing with the same person in terms of the kind of injuries that were inflicted?"

"Sounds like it. I've not come across another case that carries these hallmarks, especially the money, which adds an entirely different angle," said Cara. "I'm going to get a PM done late this afternoon, and I don't think it will take too long. I'll call you later if that's okay?"

Scott nodded and thanked her for her time.

Cara paused. "I do find this case particularly fascinating and intriguing. The money in the mouth has certainly piqued my curiosity."

"It's a strange one," replied Scott.

"Perhaps we should discuss more over a drink and swap theories?" suggested Cara.

Scott hesitated, unsure how to respond, taken aback by the sudden feeling of uncertainty.

"Erm, yes, that sounds good. We'll talk later," he replied.

19

Scott spent the afternoon doing the various admin tasks a senior officer was expected to undertake, which took time away from the recent murders that needed his attention. He didn't enjoy this part of his job. He'd much rather be out there at the coalface. He soon realised that with promotion came added rounds of meetings, an in-tray that had a mind of its own and the required supervision of junior officers.

Not forgetting the ever-increasing pressures of accountability from senior managers and the police crime commissioner, who heaped even more work upon him.

Over the last few hours, Scott had read several internal papers, flicked through police forums and digested reports relating to the changes the force was going through. He was beginning to realise the job required the tact and diplomacy of a slippery politician, to balance politics versus policing. He wasn't a political person by any means, but beneath the surface of his role was a long-standing issue in British policing. Who really controlled police tactics and policies? Where did the reasonable limits of acceptable political influence begin and end?

There continued to be considerable political controversy over several policing issues and police reform. It wasn't just police numbers and public order tactics under review, but also government cuts, the input of elected police and crime commissioners, and even the hotly contended issue of importing police chiefs from other countries.

With such a convoluted approach, any officer could question if the police had any degree of operational independence, or further still, if politics and policing needed each other to coexist for mutual benefit.

Above and beyond that, Scott had a team to supervise, a team that faced its own problems. He was down a few officers who were signed off with stress – a result of too much work and fewer resources. He was resigned to that fact, because he knew that it wasn't a localised problem. All forces were experiencing this crisis.

Scott sighed and rubbed his temples, then pushed his chair away from his desk. Turning around to face his window, he looked out over a sullen grey sky that didn't really improve his mood. Being on a high floor meant he had a decent view over the town as it sloped away from the station towards the Old Steine.

His office was at the back of the station overlooking the yard. He watched as a group of uniformed officers below piled into a public order van, no doubt heading off to patrol the busy streets of the town centre.

Scott's thoughts were interrupted by a knock on the door. He spun around, almost caught in surprise to see Raj in the doorway. Raj Singh had been with Sussex Police for the past three years. He was a well liked and trusted member of the team. A cheeky smile and practical joker. If anyone was going to pull a stunt in the office, it was Raj.

He was also responsible for the team collectively battling with their weight. Raj was a cakes and biscuits man. There'd always be some tempting treats at the end of one of the desks, proving irresistible for anyone walking by.

Raj was an officer Scott needed to supervise closely. There had been rumblings amongst the team that Raj wasn't always taking his role seriously. Raj had had the odd heated run-in with Mike over him not pulling his weight and doing the barest minimum on occasion. Mike, being a straight-talking northerner, wasn't afraid to give Raj a piece of his mind, which had led to colourful exchanges that Scott was forced to referee.

"Guv, we've just had the report from forensics regarding the first death," Raj said. "They found a hair fibre not belonging to the victim."

"Ah, okay."

Raj was animated. "Check this out, the hair fibre went through extensive cross-analysis, and it was matched to a death three years ago. A clubber by the name of Stephen Wentworth aged twenty-three. He was found unconscious outside the Urban nightclub."

Scott raised a brow in surprise. That was interesting.

"Right, Raj, fill me in as we walk. Let's get the team together. We'll stop in on Matt en route."

20

Ten minutes later, Scott and the team had gathered. There was a renewed energy in the room with the possibility of a breakthrough in the first case.

"Okay, listen up, team," Scott said. "Forensics has come back with some interesting information on the first case. Raj, do you want to carry on?"

Raj seemed to revel in the attention, all eyes on him, the team listening to his every word. This certainly played to the extrovert side of him who enjoyed the limelight.

"Thanks, guv. Okay, forensics found a match for a hair fibre they found on the first victim. The match comes back to a Stephen Wentworth, who died three years ago following an assault outside the Urban nightclub. At the time, one of the doormen" – Raj briefly paused whilst checking the file – "a Pete Tomlins, was charged with the assault. The case was dropped due to insufficient evidence. A bleed to the brain was the cause of death. There was talk at the time of witness intimidation."

"Thanks, Raj." Scott addressed the team. "We have two deaths in under a week. It looks like we're dealing with the same killer. The cause of death is almost identical. Both were stabbed in the neck; both had money stuffed in their mouths."

"Perhaps it's the fallout from a business deal gone wrong, guv?" suggested Sian.

"Could be. The cases must be linked in some way. However, we now have this hair fibre found on the first victim. If it belongs to a victim from three years ago, it's possible that whoever was there three years ago at the time of Stephen's death was also present when Edward Stone was killed."

"That's a long time in between," offered Abby.

"It is, but the money thing bothers me."

"Well, I still think it points to a business deal gone wrong, and it's some sort of payback," she said.

Scott paused for a moment and stared at the whiteboard. On it was a picture of Ed Stone and the second victim, recently identified Dave Fraser, plus the pictures of the crime scenes and the post-mortem. He turned to Abby.

"What have we got on Dave Fraser?"

"He was thirty-nine, known drugs supplier to Brighton and the surrounding area. A menacing figure, as we know. He claimed to be a legit businessman, but that never washed with anyone. He owned a small gym called Hardcore in Portland Road, Hove. Built like a brick shithouse, and when he was last nicked, it took six officers to take him down. He had convictions for possession of class B, did three years at the age of nineteen." Abby continued, "Then convicted at twenty-four, for the supply of class A, including cocaine and ecstasy. Received fourteen years for that, was due out after eight years. However, he was arranging importation of drugs, and as a result, he got a further six years for running a drug smuggling ring inside prison with hidden phones."

"A right scrote then," Scott replied.

Abby nodded and shrugged her shoulders.

"I've spoken to Matt in forensics, and as far as he's concerned, the sample analysis stands good. There's no chance of error. The DNA profile matches with Stephen Wentworth. So..." Scott paused as he gathered his thoughts. "Abby and Mike, I want you to both pull up everything we have on victims one and two. Get their bank records and download their phone logs. Also get over to Fraser's house and gym and seize any paperwork, computers, and mobile phones. If there's anything of interest, get them off to the high-tech unit; let's see what they can pull out for us."

Scott made notes as he talked. "We need to see if there's any crossover. They're both suppliers and would have been known to each other. Let's see if they were friends or foes, okay? This could be tit for tat. Sian, can you bring in Stone's fiancée tomorrow morning? We need to see how much she knows."

"Will do, guv."

"Okay, everyone, we'll call it a night. I'll update the DCI first thing in the morning, and then I'll interview Vicky Bright with Sian."

21

The PM report on Fraser hadn't come through overnight as expected. Scott made a mental note to go over to the mortuary later for the results.

His briefing with the DCI had involved a colourful exchange of words. DCI Harvey had expressed in no uncertain terms that she wanted the investigation speeded up, as they'd get a few extra brownie points with the superintendent. However, to balance out her argument, DCI Harvey was quietly pleased that two undesirables had been taken off the street, and that had saved the force considerable time and money. She was hoping that it had put a large hole in the supply chain in Brighton.

Scott liked the fact that the DCI never minced her words, but felt she was sometimes a little too close to the wind for comfort. Her political incorrectness was best left within the four walls of her office.

He'd left her room with her last comment, "Scott, get a bloody result fast," ringing in his ears.

He'd muttered, "I'll just rub my magic lamp, shall I?"

VICKY BRIGHT HAD RELUCTANTLY AGREED to come into the station. She'd protested all the way there. Sian had done her best to placate the woman, but when she hadn't shut up, Sian decided silence was her best solution to stop that droning, whiny cockney accent boring into her skull.

Vicky was seated in one of the station's interview rooms with a cup of tea. She gave Sian and Scott a glowering scowl as they sat opposite her. Sian set up the tapes in the recorder, hit the record button and did the introductory formalities.

Vicky barked at them, "Am I under arrest?" Her eyes darted from one officer to another.

Scott held up a hand to stop her from saying more.

"Ms Bright, no, you're not under arrest, you're just helping us with our enquiries into your fiancé's death. We'd also like to talk to you about the evidence we've retrieved following searches of your property and Mr Stone's clubs. However, I do need to caution you. You do not have to say anything, but it may harm your defence if you do not mention when questioned something you later rely on in court. Anything you do say may be given in evidence. Is that clear to you?"

She nodded her reply.

"For the tape, could you speak your replies, please," Sian asked.

"Yesss," she hissed.

Scott continued, "Of course, you can have legal representation should you wish, and you're perfectly entitled to leave whenever you want."

"Just get on with it," she replied impatiently.

Reciting the law seemed to pacify her venomous attack, but her glare remained fixed on the pair. Her eyes showed a cold lack of trust in those sitting opposite her.

"Ms Bright, what do you know about Edward Stone's business affairs?" Sian asked.

Vicky eyed them both with suspicion. She was either reluctant to comment or unsure as to what she should be telling them.

"Not a lot, he ran two nightclubs… successful nightclubs, I'll have you know."

"Did you know of any other business dealings that he may have been involved in?"

"Like what?"

"Anything other than his clubs… Did he have a vested interest in anything else?"

"Nope," was the curt reply back.

Scott stayed silent throughout the exchange, observing Vicky's facial expressions as Sian continued to question her.

He'd been fascinated with human behaviour since his days at university. Not long after leaving, he'd studied patterns of verbal and non-verbal communication, eye accessing cues, linguistic structures, and voice control methods – many of which had proved invaluable in recent years.

As the saying went, *The eyes are the windows to the soul. The mouth the door.* Scott never found the true origins of that saying. They'd been much debated over the years. Some attributed it to Shakespeare, others to Leonardo De Vinci and even Ralph Waldo Emerson.

He reflected that whoever had arrived at that conclusion had a fascinating perspective of human evolution. In reality the interpretation that Scott concluded for himself was that the intellect and will are seen in the eyes; the emotions, sensibilities and affections are seen in the mouth.

"Was Edward dealing in drugs?" Sian resumed.

That question lit the touchpaper and incensed the woman.

She raised her puffy eyes to meet Sian's gaze directly. She screamed, "Do you take me for some fucking idiot?" Her character changed as she leant forward, both arms spread across the table, her words accompanied by spittle rocketing from her mouth.

Sian leant back in her chair when it made contact with her cotton shirt.

Vicky continued to erupt. "Are you looking for the fucker who did this? No. Instead you're here harassing the one person who loved Eddy. How am I going to manage now?"

"I'll ask you again, was Edward dealing in drugs?" Sian repeated.

"Not as far as I know."

"So how do you explain the large quantity of class A found in your wardrobe?"

Vicky hesitated for a moment, long enough for Scott to notice. "No fucking clue, maybe he was looking after it for someone."

"That's still possession," Sian replied calmly.

"Why are you telling me? It's got nothing to do with me."

"It implicates you because you cohabit the apartment."

Vicky was clearly incensed by the accusations flying her way; her shoulders were hunched, her body curling inwards to form an imaginary cocoon.

Scott watched Vicky's responses as Sian questioned her, voice neutral. He could have jumped in and taken over, but as a junior officer, Sian needed experience and to learn how to handle a range of different reactions that she'd come across whilst interviewing witnesses and suspects.

He gauged that Vicky's outburst was either a genuine cry from the heart or a calculated attempt for sympathy. Either way, there was little they were going to get from her, but he decided to have one more throw of the dice.

He chose his words carefully. “How well did Edward know Dave Fraser?”

The question halted Vicky in her tracks. Her mind switched furiously from the verbal battle with Sian to Scott’s probing question. The momentary pause was all he needed to confirm his suspicions.

“Never heard of the bloke.”

“I think you have, Vicky,” he challenged in a firm, direct voice. “I reckon you know him very well.”

“What? You Derren Brown or something?”

Scott slammed his hand on the table. Both Vicky and Sian jumped in their chairs.

He glared at the woman. “No, I’m Detective Inspector Baker, and you’re pissing me off. I’m here to catch the ‘fucker’, as you put it, the man who killed your Eddy, so if you don’t help, I’ll assume you’re withholding information and obstructing a murder investigation.”

His words were firm, his eyes locked in a battle of wills with Vicky’s. Scott wasn’t going to let this one go. Her eyes were giving him all the information he needed.

There was an extended silence as neither side budged.

Then Vicky’s eyes flickered just a little. “I don’t know him, but I heard Eddy having a row with him on the phone a few weeks ago.”

Scott frowned. “A row? What do you mean?”

Vicky shook her head.

“Did they often speak on the phone or meet up?”

“Not as far as I know. I never heard him talk about the bloke, and I never met him.”

“Was Dave Fraser supplying the drugs we found in your wardrobe?”

“No... no... no...” was the reply. She kept shaking her head. “Eddy wasn’t into drugs.”

"So how did they get there? Early Christmas present from Santa?"

Frustration got the better of her. Vicky shifted around in her chair, crossing her arms and then uncrossing them. Her pupils were dilating, a sure sign that her brain was working hard.

His suspicion was confirmed when she covered her eyes with one hand. Scott knew from his human behaviour training that people often covered their eyes or mouths when letting out an untruth, to either cover up a lie or hide their reaction to it.

Sian scribbled away on her notepad, capturing Vicky's responses.

"Are you sure you're not holding back?" Scott pushed. "You see, I think you're not being totally honest with me."

Vicky tutted and looked up towards the ceiling, her eyes welling up again.

"No." Her voice broke as her chin trembled. "Look, I never met the guy. All I know is he had an argument with my Eddy on the phone..." She trailed off.

Scott concluded the interview soon after and arranged for Vicky to be taken home.

"Didn't get much, did we, guv?" asked Sian as they walked back up to the office.

"Far from it, Sian. We got exactly what we needed."

22

The case bothered Scott. He knew he wasn't far from making the connections that the DCI wanted, but was still missing the crucial link. He decided to accompany Mike and Abby to the search of Dave Fraser's house.

Reynolds Road was just an ordinary unassuming suburban street, with a mixture of average semi-detached and detached properties. As Scott got out of his car, he noticed how one side of the street was predominately semi-detached residences, and the other side of the road was mainly detached properties.

Dave Fraser's property was a detached house with white UPVC double-glazed bay-fronted windows. It had a small front garden with off-street parking and a quirky little single window in the roof space.

The officer standing by the front door was PC Oju, whom Scott had met outside The Phoenix nightclub. They both nodded at each other as Scott stepped inside. The house had been lavishly decorated with cream leather sofas in the lounge and a giant sixty-inch curved HDTV that took pride of place on one wall. Scott thought the TV was way too large for the room as he continued to walk around the ground floor. The kitchen looked newly fitted with marble tops and Shaker-style units.

"Business must be booming. I must buy myself a gym," Scott muttered as he looked around the empty kitchen, running his finger along the cold smoothness of the marble top.

Abby walked in holding up an evidence bag.

"There's just over eight and a half grand in here."

"Hardly pin money, is it?" Scott replied.

"Hardly, and Mike's just found about another five grand in the back bedroom behind a wardrobe."

The property search continued for the afternoon and yielded lots of potential evidence and clues. Amongst the items documented and bagged were £13,725 in cash, two laptops, three mobile phones, and a book with times and dates. Scott assumed the times and dates were related to suspect transactions.

A crucial discovery was what appeared to be an identical black holdall to the one recovered from Ed Stone's property. It contained several large, clear bags of white powder, which, once tested, would no doubt be confirmed as a class A substance. This last find led to Scott calling in the sniffer dog to give the property a once-over in case anything had been missed.

Scott was back in the office by late afternoon, going over the records he'd requested for both victims. He'd hardly eaten all day and was munching on a tuna mayo baguette he'd grabbed from the canteen. It tasted bland, and the bread felt like it was a few days past its sell-by date, making each mouthful dry and hard to swallow.

He hankered after a hot meal, but the meals at the station were dubious at the best of times. The only thing they seemed to do well was a good breakfast dripping in fat.

On the odd occasion, Scott had experienced the infamous gut-buster breakfast at the twenty-four-hour Market Diner, which was around the corner from the station. Despite valiant attempts to avoid the place, Scott had relented because it was one of Mike's favourite hovels. He'd often stared in amazement at Mike, who could polish off a fry-up in minutes, using a slice of white bread to mop up the remnants of his baked beans sauce and egg yolk. It had left Scott believing that each breakfast was knocking at least one year off his life, whilst adding an extra inch to his waistline. Mike was a living testimony to that theory.

Scott stopped mid-mouthful when he noticed something in the bank records of both victims going back over the past five years. He scanned left to right, from one sheet to another. The closer he looked, the faster his mind buzzed, trying to make sense of what he was seeing. There was a series of regular payments over the years going from Dave Fraser to Ed Stone's account. They weren't small sums either. Scott counted over twenty-five payments of between four and seven thousand pounds.

He could reasonably explain it as legitimate business transfers that happen millions of times a day in the banking system. However, the fact that the two people in question both had convictions and were dead piqued his interest.

Scott grabbed his calculator and worked out some figures. He whistled low when he realised that at least £130k had been paid to Ed Stone over the past five years. That in itself warranted further scrutiny, but what interested him most was what he found going back to an earlier statement: a large entry of seventy-six thousand pounds paid to Stone from Fraser.

Scott's heart thumped in his chest. He sat upright in his chair. Scenarios were flashing in his mind. Both victims knew each other and were involved in some type of deal. He started to question his own assumption.

Did we have it wrong all this time?

Was it in fact Stone who was a bigger fish and had been supplying to Fraser?

Had they got in too deep with an unknown third party, and things had turned sour?

Scott also had to consider another possibility. With increased freedom of movement amongst EU citizens, a distinct lack of border controls, rising immigration and the financial strength of the City of London, there had been a rise of cross-border organised crime.

Recently, criminal gangs from both the UK and Eastern Europe had expanded operations to the south coast to exploit the many entry points it had to offer. This had become an area of concern for Sussex Police.

So perhaps they pissed off the wrong guys. If Eastern European gangs are involved, then Stone and Fraser may have been way out of their league.

He'd only just read a report from Europol that as many as 1,500 gangs were actively targeting the UK, with the cocaine and heroin markets here ranked amongst the highest in Europe. So it was plausible that Stone and Fraser had got in too deep, or tried to rip someone off, or even just been eliminated to reduce the competition.

Scott had these thoughts and many more rolling around inside his mind as he figured out what steps to take next.

23

The sun sat low in the sky as Scott drove along the seafront. It was a crisp morning; the sea was still; the pavements were covered in a pure-white sheet of frost that glistened in the sunlight. Even on a cold, crisp sunny morning, Brighton was magical.

There was the usual throng of people heading off to work mixed in with the early rising tourists taking photos along the seafront, keen to capture the essence of Brighton with Palace Pier in the background.

It was views like this that reminded Scott of all the reasons he'd moved away from bigger cities like London and Essex. Out here there was freedom, fresh air and space. Even though his caseload was just as busy, being in Brighton and experiencing the laid-back atmosphere of the town helped to balance out the stresses and difficulties that the job placed on him.

He made his way over to Lewes Road. His first call was to stop in and see Cara to get an update on the post-mortem that she'd conducted.

He made his way to the mortuary entrance, pausing to allow a middle-aged lady to go first. She was accompanied by a younger man who had his arm around her. Sadly, he'd seen this scenario many times, the family of a deceased person coming to formally identify their loved ones or see them in the chapel of rest.

Scott stood back, giving them space as they waited for a mortuary technician to let them in.

A few moments later one did, and he followed through the same entrance. He showed his badge. The mortuary technician acknowledged Scott with a nod as he carried on consoling the family. Scott headed to the observation room. He saw Cara busy at work on the body of a young female perhaps no older than seventeen or eighteen.

Though he dealt with the hard end of life, he held a degree of respect for a pathologist's job. In Scott's eyes, the deceased was still a person, someone's mother, father, daughter, son, brother or sister. However, he guessed from Cara's perspective, they were just a body. A time capsule that she needed to open, dissect and examine to ascertain the cause of death, without adding any emotional component.

He pressed the intercom buzzer to get Cara's attention. She paused midway to look up, her hands occupied with the dark red liver of the female.

"Detective Inspector, what a pleasant surprise. Why don't you get kitted up and join me?" she said, smiling behind her plastic face visor.

Scott groaned under a false smile. Much as he was looking forward to seeing Cara, she had a knack of making his stomach lurch at the mere mention of joining her in the examination room. He shuffled along begrudgingly, like a child being forced to attend a compulsory maths lesson, finally entering the preparation room to get gowned up.

"Hard at work already, Dr Hall?"

"Well, if you can call being elbow-deep in blood and the innards of a corpse hard work, then I have to agree with you, Inspector."

Scott gave the smallest of smiles. "I was expecting the PM report yesterday. Considering I haven't received it yet, I thought I'd stop in first to gather your thoughts before heading off to the station. What can you tell me?"

"Ah yes, I'm really sorry. The report's done; I just didn't get the time to email it over to you. Had a bit of a rush job here yesterday afternoon." She looked down at the girl on the metal table in front of her. She had a thin frame, blonde hair and was a natural beauty. "Three teenagers died in a car on the A27 near Polegate. Looks like all three were off their faces on cannabis when they lost control and went off the road. This poor girl is the third of the victims. What a poor waste of life."

She straightened up. "Anyway, back to business. Come over to this table, and we can look at your man." Cara pointed to the middle examination table, where a light blue sheet covered the distinctive outline of a body.

She pulled back the sheet to reveal Dave Fraser. The front of his torso had a purple-red discolouration where the blood had settled after he had been killed. Scott knew this to be livor mortis, having attended many PMs in recent years. The patchwork Y of stitches extended from his collarbones down to his pubic bone.

"Long or short version?" Cara asked.

"Short version will do for now, and I can read your report later."

"Estimated time of death is between midnight and four a.m. He was stabbed twice in the neck."

"Same type of blade?"

Cara nodded. "My guess is yes. It's a bit messy in comparison to the first victim, but only because of the second stab wound. Again, the knife pierced the neck. Having looked deeper into the neck cavity, it appears that the knife was thrust in and then pushed in a further inch up to the blade hilt. The piercing had a smooth edge and a rough torn edge like the first victim. My guess is it's the same type of survival blade. Then it looks like the blade was pulled out, taking some tissue with it.

"What's different on this occasion is that he has a similar, large stab wound in his left hand. If I had to guess, I'd say that the victim brought his hand up to shield himself or reach for the wound, and the attacker stabbed him again, trapping the victim's hand. It's messy, and the second entry point is much larger and disturbed. The knife severed the sternothryroid and onohyoid neck muscles. This was a far more violent attack." Her last few words hung in the air.

Cara looked at Scott whilst he stared at the corpse, lost in thought, his mind searching for answers and clues. The room had an air of desolation to it. A cold tingle raced down his back, and Scott was jolted out of his inner world. He felt as if the temperature of the room had dropped a few degrees, even though it hadn't, and it was most likely due to his fear.

Scott exhaled hard before looking at Cara. "Thanks, Dr Hall. That's been enlightening to say the least. These two crimes are connected because the victims knew each other."

"Really?"

"Yep, I just need to find out who they pissed off."

"We've got several hair fibres from this victim, and they're currently being analysed. In fact, I'm expecting the results within the next few days, so I'll get that to you as soon as I can," Cara offered reassuringly. "Have you got any theories that you care to share?"

"A few," he replied. "Well, perhaps one."

"How about we discuss it over a drink this evening? We could grab some pub grub too if we're hungry. It gets pretty lonely doing this job, hardly a lot of banter among the dead," she said, waving around the room.

Scott paused for a moment, unsure; then he agreed to the idea.

"Great! How about the Cricketers in Black Lion Street at seven p.m.?" she suggested.

"Sounds good to me, Dr Hall. I'll see you then." He was walking to the door whilst removing his face mask when Cara called out to him. Scott looked over his shoulder.

"And call me Cara, DCI Baker," she said, wagging a finger at him in jest.

"Then call me Scott," he said in return.

SCOTT SPENT the next few hours tied up in meetings with DCI Harvey and the superintendent, updating them both on the cases. They were joined by the press officer to formulate a press release on the second victim and an appeal for information on both cases that would be going out tomorrow.

Lunchtime came and went, and Scott had just enough time to grab a tuna sandwich and fruit juice from the vending machine before sitting down to go through the report the high-tech unit had left on his desk.

Scott made a mental note to get one of the team to start working through Stone's contact list. There were five numbers that Stone called regularly. Scott figured one would be Vicky Bright. The others needed closer scrutiny. He had a hunch that one of the others would be Fraser.

The laptop report came back clean. According to the high-tech team, it was a Sony Vaio Core i7 2.00GHz with 8GB

RAM, running on a 64-bit operating system. The description made as much sense to him as the theory of relativity.

The laptop was being used for club purposes with folders set up for income and expenditure, promotion and marketing, staffing and payroll. There were email folders relating to Google email addresses for both nightclubs. Attempts had been made to delete the browsing history and some files. The high-tech team had managed to retrieve some of the data, but work was still ongoing to complete that task.

Scott spotted that the deleted history included pages for plane arrival times at Gatwick Airport, Newhaven Ferry Port timetables, the British Microlight Aircraft Association, and a Google search for farm landing strips and Shoreham airport. This looked like background research for planned operations for the importation of drugs.

This has to be drugs related now.

He gathered up his notes and the file, with the intention to go through it more thoroughly tonight at home. In the meantime, he had plans to meet Cara at seven p.m., which meant he had enough time to grab his running gear and head out for a quick run along Marine Parade to Roedean and back.

24

The Cricketers was set off the seafront amidst the bustle of restaurants, bars and coffee shops. It was a popular pub with a dark red Victorian interior. Scott noticed everything was a shade of red: the carpets, the well-worn seating and the floral-textured, dark red wallpaper.

Whilst waiting for Cara to arrive, he ordered himself a bottle of Beck's and spent a few moments staring with curiosity at how every inch of the walls and ceiling was decorated with framed pictures of people from a bygone era, along with mounted stuffed deer heads and gold plates.

What amused Scott was the line of china chamber pots that hung from a beam across the bar, which added to the quirkiness and atmosphere. It was one of Brighton's hidden treasures and tucked away so well that many tourists missed it.

No sooner had that thought crossed his mind, he felt a tap on his shoulder. Turning, he did a double take.

"Almost didn't recognise you without your clothes on..." Scott remarked as he stood to greet Cara. She wore a navy blue, short-sleeved, figure-hugging dress. Her long and straight dark brown hair cascaded over her shoulders and down the front of her chest. Her dark brown eyes were warm and inviting.

"Excuse me?"

"Sorry, I meant your scrubs," Scott backtracked in embarrassment.

"I'll take that as a compliment, kind sir." She mock bowed.

He laughed and tried to think of something quick and witty to say, but his mind went blank.

He felt brave enough to try another comment. "You look stunning."

"It comes easy," she replied, shrugging and flicking her hair back with one hand, in a mock gesture of self-adulation. "You could have made an effort, too." She looked him up and down.

"Erm, sorry, I..."

She laughed. "I'm joking, Scott!"

He smiled. "I'll have you know that this is a Paul Smith suit."

"You sure it's not a suit from a vintage shop in the North Laines?" Cara teased.

"Cheeky mare." He pointed at the bar. "Do you see anyone else splitting their sides with laughter?"

Cara calmed herself. "You know I'm just pulling your leg, but you're an easy target."

"I'll remember to dress in a black bin liner next time."

"Who says there'll be a next time?"

"Fair point."

"Well, if you do, make sure there's nothing under it." She winked.

They both laughed. He liked her sense of humour. Laughter had been missing from his life in recent years. At least Cara was good at breaking the ice; it saved him having to do it.

After getting Cara a large Cabernet Sauvignon and a beer for himself, they grabbed a table towards the back of the bar and sat opposite each other. He opted for the uncomfortable bar stool, whilst giving her the comfy seat against the wall.

"How's the case going?" Cara asked.

"The term *slowly but surely* comes to mind. I've made some inroads, but I'm still missing the breakthrough. We're certain the victims knew each other, but why they were murdered is still unknown."

She took a large gulp of wine and breathed out a sigh of relaxation. She closed her eyes for a brief second to relish the feeling as the wine clearly hit the spot.

"Is this one taxing you, then?" Cara continued.

"Just a bit. I've had murder cases before, but multiple connected murders are new to me. The DCI's been helpful, but I'm the SIO on the case."

"What's your theory?"

"My hunch is that the victims got in over their heads with another drugs supplier. I can't see another reason at the moment."

"What's the deal with the money in the mouth?" questioned Cara.

"Not sure. Perhaps they stitched someone up or stole their money, and the killer left notes to suggest that you can have their cash but only when you're dead." Scott shrugged and held out his hands.

"That's plausible." She nodded. "But why not just kill them? Why leave a calling card of some sort? I think there's more to it, personally."

"True, but it's early days. The investigation's starting to get some traction, and with the fibre from the first victim matching someone who died three years ago, it opens up a different avenue for us. It could be connected or a pure coincidence."

Cara pretended to stifle a yawn. "So we going to talk shop all night?"

"Erm, didn't you suggest a drink to discuss theories?"

She held up a hand in mock submission. "Guilty, your honour."

They switched topics, and the conversation flowed comfortably between them. They discussed the places they'd visited, favourite foods and what they did in their spare time.

Scott took a swig of his beer. "Anyway, so tell me, why pathology? It's a pretty grim role. Hardly a conversation starter at a party, and certainly no one around to laugh at your lame jokes."

She rolled her eyes. "My dad was a doctor, and Mum was a nurse. They're both retired now and live in London. In my teens I was fascinated by weird stuff, like paranormal things, zombies and death. I remember loving dissections in my biology A-level class. The mouse, the frog, the sheep's eye... I was engrossed in them. People thought I was weird then... They probably still think that."

She laughed and took a sip of wine.

Scott was amazed at Cara's ability to talk with ease. It was a side to her he found refreshing.

Cara carried on. "It just felt right to go into medicine and then specialise in pathology." She stared into empty space for a moment. "Then I moved from London to this post in Brighton a year ago. It certainly made the parents happy... How about you?"

"Well, I just fell into the police force, I guess, after university. I wasn't sure what I wanted to do. But it offered a career, and having been to a police recruitment evening, I soon realised that no two days would be the same, and that meant variety. A desk job didn't appeal to me, and the thought of trudging into London on the Tube every day put me off."

"So why Brighton if you were in Essex?" Cara asked.

"I fell in love with Brighton when I was studying here. I loved the pace of life, the vibrancy of the town, the people, and I loved being by the sea. The crime caseload here is different compared to Essex and London."

"Until now," Cara interrupted.

"Until now." Scott nodded in agreement. "Listen, I'm going to have to shoot now. I've got to go over the case file this evening. Dull, I know, but I need to." He shrugged as he drained his beer.

Cara looked a little disappointed, but accepted his reason, finishing her wine with a hefty glug.

"Well, it's been a lovely evening," she said. "It's great just getting out and having a drink and chat. We should do this again."

"That would be nice," Scott acknowledged.

They said their goodbyes with a brief kiss on the cheek.

On his short drive home Scott reflected on what he'd been missing, and that was company. His life over the last few years had been a mixture of work, the gym, solitary time at home – which he hated – and walking along the beach people-watching. In fact, Scott had thrown himself into work just to keep his mind occupied.

But the alternative wasn't worth considering.

He only had one option, and that was to look forward, because looking back was too painful.

25

Scott was back there again, watching it unfold in front of him. He'd been across the street waiting for them when it happened. He'd only turned his head for a moment, but that moment changed his life forever, extinguished the flame of contentment and happiness that had given him so much joy.

He ran, but his legs felt like they were stuck in quicksand, each step painfully slow, each second feeling like a minute. The scene unfolded in front of him like a movie on the big screen. Scott was a spectator, powerless to change the outcome.

It was getting darker, and the wind started swirling around him, throwing up dust, making it harder to see the carnage. Scott fell to his knees, crying, screaming, his eyes wide with horror and disbelief, his mouth unable to form any words. Saliva formed bubbles as he tried to breathe.

"Why?" he cried, looking to the sky, hoping for some divine explanation. "Why, why, why?"

Scott woke from his nightmare and released a hollering cry. "NOOO!"

He looked around his dark bedroom, trying to see more than the blankness of the room. His heart pounded in his chest; his pulse thumped in his ears, his breathing laboured. It took a few moments to calm down. He wiped the sweat from his forehead.

He hated the nightmares; they left him exhausted and in a place he didn't want to visit.

His bedside clock glowed a bright five twenty-four a.m. Unable to fall asleep again, he decided to get up, make himself a coffee and watch the early morning Sky news. But as Scott sat on the sofa, he went back over the nightmare once again.

The nightmares were more frequent, disturbing and dark after he'd had a drink. He wondered if the alcohol relaxed him so much that his mind and body were unable to hold back the memories that he did so well to contain during consciousness.

SCOTT SAT in the briefing room shortly after eight a.m., finishing a breakfast of mixed fruits and Greek yogurt whilst waiting for the rest of the team to arrive. Raj and Sian were already there, with Mike trailing in apologetically last.

Scott perched on the end of the table.

"Morning, ladies," Scott started off, his opening comment met with the deliberate clearing of throats from Raj and Mike.

Scott smiled and carried on. "As I said, morning, ladies. We've got work to do." He looked around. "Where's Abby, Mike?"

"Guv, she's just on the phone to officers in Southampton. She's been digging around in Fraser's background. She'll be joining us shortly."

"Okay, well, let's carry on. We know that Stone and Fraser knew each other, and we know that Fraser was giving Stone a lot of money, possibly in exchange for drugs. We also know that Stone was more than likely importing drugs. The high-tech unit retrieved deleted web history relating to ferry timetables, landing strips and so on." He looked at his junior officer. "Sian, I want you to go through the list of contacts on Stone's phone. Five numbers crop up the most. Find out who they belong to. One of them must be his supplier."

Sian nodded her agreement.

"Raj, I want you to get hold of the CCTV footage of both clubs for the last few weeks. Let's see if we can get Fraser in the frame or identify any contact between them, okay?"

"Yep."

Scott got up, readying to walk over to the window.

Mike raised his pen to get his attention. "Guv, I've been chasing up a few contacts and asking about the Phoenix and Urban. Now I'm not sure how much truth there is in it, but a few said that Fraser was a main dealer, and none of them had known of Stone dealing. If you wanted some gear, his clubs were the place to get them hassle-free."

Scott stood in silence, deep in thought. The team exchanged glances and raised brows, as if having a telepathic conversation between themselves.

The penny dropped, and Scott spun around. He slapped his forehead with the palm of his hand.

"Bollocks, I think I've been looking at this from the wrong angle."

Mike frowned. "You've lost me, guv."

"Mike, Fraser is the main dealer. I reckon he was paying Stone a sweetener in return for peddling his gear in the clubs hassle-free. The regular payments make sense now."

There was a general agreement around the room.

Mike said, "But that doesn't account for the seventy-six grand paid to Stone a few years ago."

"Hang on, guv," Sian interrupted, quickly sifting through her notes. "Okay, how about this? Our investigations into Stone have already shown that he launched both clubs about five years ago. What if Fraser helped fund the clubs, and that seventy-six grand was his share of the business? The timing of the payment seems to make sense." She checked more notes. "That plus regular payments in return for using the clubs to peddle his gear. That makes Fraser a silent partner. I've checked, and he doesn't own shares in the business, nor were there any loans made to him as far as I can tell."

"Sounds about right, guv," said Mike.

Scott nodded. "And it was a lucrative set-up that someone else wanted to get in on, resulting in them both being taken out... good work, Sian."

"Thanks, guv."

Scott was about to carry on when Abby burst into the briefing room, out of breath.

"Guv, sorry I'm late. I just got off the phone to officers in Southampton. They were dealing with a case a while back involving Fraser. He was the victim of a shooting, looked like attempted murder."

She caught her breath. "They charged another known supplier by the name of Lee Stubbins and his brother Luke for the crime. Lee's in Pentonville serving fourteen years, but his brother absconded from custody and was never captured. Lee's still a pretty big drug dealer in the South East and, even though he's behind bars, is still running things and trying to muscle in on the Brighton drugs scene. He already has operations in Bournemouth, Eastbourne and Southampton. Our colleagues in Southampton have current intel that he wants greater control of the south coast supply and distribution chain."

This sounded promising. Scott rubbed his hands together. He needed to find out who wanted control badly enough to kill them.

He looked at his team. "Mike, once Raj has got the CCTV for both clubs, go through them and look for Fraser. Also look for anyone going in the back door of both clubs. There may have been meetings with whoever wanted to muscle in. Can you cross-check with records on the database, latest intelligence on the movers and shakers in the drugs scene, and see what you can find? It's likely we may have the killer captured on video."

"Perhaps they refused to agree to a deal and, well, we know the ending," added Sian.

Scott was thinking hard. "It's certainly worth exploring, and it's all we've got at the moment. Let's crack on, and I'll update the DCI later. We'll have a briefing update tonight. In the meantime, Abby, you and I need to head to London to have a chat with Lee Stubbins. Can you phone ahead and inform the governor that we need to interview Stubbins?"

"On it now, guv."

26

The fifty-minute train journey to London flew by. Abby fell asleep not long after the train had left Brighton. Scott put that down to her being up much of the night with her youngest, who'd been unwell.

As the countryside breezed past him, Scott spent his time listening to tracks on his phone, dozing for a few moments, and running through the case in his mind. He sensed he was getting closer to a breakthrough; he just wasn't sure what form that would take.

Visiting Stubbins was a long shot, but if he'd tried to kill Fraser once, then he could have arranged for a second hit. But that wouldn't explain Stone being taken out. Scott wondered what the connection might be between Stone and Stubbins.

As he and Abby stood at the visitors' entrance to Pentonville, Scott couldn't help but admire the tall walls of this Victorian prison. The first big prison in London, it was now an institution with outdated facilities, extreme overcrowding and rat infestations, and deemed not fit for purpose in recent reviews.

Scott had been to Pentonville on a few occasions. Like any visit by a police officer, his presence was often met with aggressive chanting from inmates and threats of the lewd sexual acts they were going to inflict on the officer's loved ones.

The interview room was a cold solitary place, with white walls and a grey floor. A ceiling strip light encased in a wire cage, a metal table and four chairs screwed to the floor, and bars over a frosted-glass window were poignant reminders of their location. The Ritz it was certainly not.

Scott and Abby sat side by side; they had agreed on the train that Abby would lead and Scott would step in if needed.

The metal door opened, and a short, muscular man walked in, accompanied by two prison officers. They stood by the entrance once the door was shut, allowing Stubbins to seat himself.

Scott noticed how Stubbins's eyes shifted from Abby to him, but his expression offered no hint of what he was thinking or feeling. He locked his gaze on Abby.

Abby spoke. "I'm Detective Sergeant Trent, and this is Detective Inspector Baker."

Stubbins didn't shift his steely gaze from her. "Do I need a brief?" he asked with a deep, measured drawl.

"Well, that depends on if you've done anything wrong, Mr Stubbins," Abby replied.

He smiled slightly. "Me? I'm a saint in here, your model inmate." He looked briefly around the room they were in.

Stubbins looked back, and his gaze locked on Abby once again. His face was expressionless but menacing at the same time. Scott noticed the attention left Abby somewhat uncomfortable, but then she regained her confidence.

"We need you to help us with our enquiries on an ongoing case."

"The police needing my help?" he said sarcastically, then bellowed with laughter. "I'm honoured, but you'll get fuck all from me."

He almost spit his last words out as he leant forward aggressively, catching Abby, Scott and the guards on the hop. The guards took a few steps forward in readiness, but they were not needed.

Abby continued, "When's the last time you or your associates had any contact with Dave Fraser?"

"No comment."

"Have you made any death threats towards Dave Fraser?"

"No comment."

Stubbins was bulky and muscular – the result of years of pumping iron. Stubble for a beard, and a shaved head. His dark brown eyes displayed hatred on all levels. Scott imagined that he struck fear in those who crossed him.

He leant in towards the table. "Dave Fraser was killed a few days ago."

Stubbins's face broke into a small smile; he pursed his lips. "I know. Good news travels fast. I need to shake the hand of the fucker who beat me to it."

"You going to shake your own hand, then?" Scott suggested.

The question was met with a cold stare. "Nothing to do with me."

"You see, I think you wanted Fraser's patch. You tried to take him out and failed... miserably," Scott said, hanging on the last word, much to Stubbins's irritation. "So you arranged for him to be taken out, leaving you in the clear here."

"No comment."

"Do you know Edward Stone?"

"No comment."

"Do you know how to spell comment?" Scott asked, trying to unsettle Stubbins and get a reaction from him, but he didn't take the bait. He sat there, his gaze on Abby, his eyes moving between her face and her breasts.

Scott continued, "Did you know Stone's dead too, killed the same way."

That question was met with silence. Scott knew that Stubbins wasn't going to shift, but he needed to rattle the inmate's cage.

"Where's your brother Luke? Did you get the word out to him to do your dirty work? Is he still in Brighton or sunning it in the Costas using *your* money? Perhaps he's even shagging your missus?" Scott fixed his stare, looking for the slightest reaction. But Stubbins remained unfazed by the questions.

Scott wanted to pick up his chair and wrap it round the arrogant fucker's head. But there was a need for protocol and patience.

Scott leant forward, keeping his frustration in check. "Do you know something, Lee? I'm going to find the evidence to link you to both of their murders, and you're going to spend a very... very... long... time at Her Majesty's pleasure."

Scott noticed a faint flicker in Stubbins's eyes. The man had maintained his cool unfazed look. To any observer Stubbins was unaffected by Scott's last comment, but he knew differently. His understanding of eye accessing cues confirmed that he'd got to the inmate. The flicker was fear; the flicker was Stubbins panicking.

Stubbins broke off his stare and turned to Scott. "You've got this so wrong that I feel sorry for you. There's only one brain cell between the two of you, and even that's not working." He spoke slow and measured.

He then turned to Abby and leered at her, holding onto his bravado. "I bet you're a great fuck in bed."

Abby replied calmly, "You'll never know."

With that, both officers rose and made their way out of the interview room, with the sound of Stubbins swearing behind them.

No sooner had Abby left the room, her chest heaved, and she blew out a sigh of relief. "I don't like him, guv. Arrogant tosser."

"Me neither."

ON THE TRAIN journey back home, the pair discussed the case. Theories were tossed back and forth. Scott had a feeling that Stubbins was involved in some way; the hard bit was going to be proving it.

Another alert from the high-tech unit flashed up on Scott's phone. After opening the email, he skimmed through the report. There were two documents: one for Fraser's three phones and the other for his two laptops.

He also opened their previous reports on Stone's equipment. As Scott had hoped, there was heavy call traffic between the two men. Fraser's laptops were clean, but his Twitter account had lots of cryptic messages that were sent between himself using the username Meaty, and three other accounts with the usernames Dropship, Glitterball and Timetraveller.

Scott believed that the other usernames could lead back to the key players in Fraser's supply and distribution chain. Finding out who they were would be a harder task.

He took a wild guess that Dropship probably dropped off the goods, Timetraveller was the courier, but he didn't have a clue who Glitterball was. Scott made a mental note to check if the high-tech team had found any evidence of Twitter activity on Stone's devices, as he hadn't seen it noted in the earlier report.

Scott forwarded the new report on to Sian, asking her to investigate Stubbins's background in more detail. He also instructed her to contact Twitter and see if they could identify the usernames.

He knew that getting the names would be hard, due to Twitter's data protection rules. Last time he'd tried to obtain user data, he was informed that it would involve lengthy and expensive legal proceedings and a court order from a Californian court. That was enough to put Scott off. But he had to try again.

27

Three days had passed since Fraser's murder and a week since Stone's. Scott was confident that the pieces of the jigsaw were falling into place. Progress was still too slow for the DCI and superintendent, who were the ones in the media eye and were experiencing more pressure than him to get results.

Raj and Mike had spent hours trawling through CCTV footage of both the Urban and Phoenix clubs and had identified grainy footage of Fraser entering the back of the Phoenix. In the footage, Fraser was carrying large holdalls that looked identical to the one found in his house. The good news was that Fraser was seen leaving the club empty-handed, which confirmed Scott's theory that he was the dealer in all of this.

His theory was further validated when forensics confirmed that the traces of white powder found in Stone's office and other areas of the club were cocaine and chemically matched the white powder found at Fraser's property.

What piqued Scott's interest was the evidence of PCP and ice at the Urban, both class A drugs. Scott was alarmed to read how ice, commonly known as crystal meth, was starting to find its way onto the drug scene locally. He'd only ever come across it once before in a raid, when officers from Essex had been drafted into a three-hundred-officer drugs raid on an estate in Tower Hamlets.

With the reports from forensics and the high-tech unit sprawled out over his desk, he scribbled away conclusions on his notepad. He wrote out the names of the deceased, their associates, the clubs, the type of drugs and drew directional lines between them, with sporadic question marks everywhere.

With his head full of facts, figures and theories, Scott could now confirm that Fraser was indeed the supplier. A major supplier at that if he was now bringing in PCP and crystal meth. With Fraser out of the equation, Scott wondered if the supply chain had taken a huge hit, something that would come as a relief to the Sussex force.

The fact that the manufacture and distribution of PCP and crystal meth was a highly lucrative business meant it was likely someone else wanted control of its local supply chain.

He kept coming back to Lee Stubbins. Scott was sure he had a bigger part to play in this, but with a lack of cooperation from the man, he'd need to gather more intel before fully understanding his involvement. With the press release out on Fraser's murder and a wider appeal on both deaths, Scott was hopeful that further information would come to light.

Scott's concentration was interrupted when Raj burst through his office door, both out of breath and excited.

"Don't you ever knock, Raj?" Scott said in startled shock.

"I'm sorry, guv. My apologies." He smiled.

"It's fine, I should have shut my door whilst going through this stuff," Scott said as he waved his hand over his desk. "What's happened?"

"Déjà vu, guv. Results are back on the analysis from the hair fibres found by the path. We have a positive ID for the fibre found on the second victim, Fraser. Check this out, because it gets better... It's a match for the one found on Stone." Raj paused for effect before continuing, "It belongs to the victim from three years ago, the clubber who was killed."

Scott raised a brow and stared at his scribbles. The one person he'd failed to add to his page was Stephen Wentworth.

"Right, where's Abby?"

"Abby's got a few hours off... taking her kid to the doctor or something. She's not back till four p.m."

"In that case get Mike to pull the file for Stephen Wentworth immediately."

"Mike's a step ahead of you, guv. He's printed it off and is on the way to you now."

Scott swivelled his chair to look out the window and reflect on the news, trying to tie up further loose ends. "It looks like the same person who was there when Stephen was killed was present at both of our murders," he muttered as he vocalised his thoughts.

"A friend of Stephen's who came in contact with him? Revenge maybe?" Raj offered.

"That's plausible, but I can't imagine hair fibres remaining intact for over three years, which would mean that the clothes this person wore three years ago hadn't been washed since."

At that moment Mike's reflection loomed into view as he poked his head around the corner. "Okay to come in, guv?"

Scott turned, giving Raj a look of *So that's how you come into my office now?* Raj looked sheepishly down at his shoes and the floor – in fact anywhere other than at Scott.

"Okay, Mike, what have we got?"

Mike entered the office. "Stephen Wentworth was killed outside the Urban nightclub three years ago. Charges were brought against the doormen at the time, but the case was dropped due to insufficient evidence. There was talk of witness intimidation, but the case was never followed through, guv."

"I want you and Abby to dig deeper into the Stephen Wentworth case. We need to cover all angles," said Scott. "We could be looking for someone who was close to Stephen at the time of his death. Look at his family, his friends and see if there's anything worth chasing up. Get back to me with an update."

"Will do."

With that, Raj and Mike shot off.

No sooner had the officers left his office, DCI Harvey ambled in.

"Any updates, Scott?"

With progress being so slow, he knew the DCI wanted answers quickly. Anything other than good news wouldn't be welcomed.

Scott ran a hand through his hair and arched his back to stretch. "We have two deceased. Fraser was a silent partner in Stone's club, and in return for a monthly retainer, Stone allowed Fraser to peddle his drugs. We also have a hair fibre on both victims that matches a clubber who died following an incident outside the Urban nightclub three years ago."

"Someone was present at both of these murders who was around three years ago outside the Urban?"

"Correct, ma'am. We have a potential suspect seen in the vicinity of the second murder, but unfortunately the description's vague, and we've got nothing to go on from the recent press releases either."

The DCI huffed and pursed her lips in dissatisfaction.

Scott added, "However, DS Trent and I interviewed Lee

Stubbins in prison, and I've a feeling he's connected in some way. He was put away for the attempted murder of Fraser. The two lines of enquiry we're following are backgrounds on both the clubber Stephen Wentworth and Lee Stubbins."

"Okay, keep me informed. And let me know if you need anything," she offered as a parting comment. DCI Harvey left his office.

The case perplexed Scott. He stared at several possibilities on his notepad but needed a breakthrough soon. Tiredness hit, and he rubbed his temples. He needed to clear his head and get some space.

But first, he fired off an email to the forensics team, asking for double confirmation on the hair fibre match. He needed to be one hundred per cent confident in the decisions and actions he took next.

SCOTT DROVE down the Kingsway and parked up by Hove lawns. It was a cool but bright spring evening. Brighton looked picturesque in the evening sun, with the regal white-washed period town houses of Brunswick Terrace to one side and the beach opposite, framing the view.

Scott spent the next hour walking along the beach, clearing his head. He found the scenery both mesmerising and relaxing. He noticed a few others enjoying walks a short distance away, dogs jumping in and out of the sea without a care in the world.

He watched two young ladies walking barefoot over the stones, laughing and screeching as the cold water raced around their ankles. Scott didn't know how others managed that. Whenever he'd tried to walk over the stones, he'd hobbled, every step more painful than the last.

He glanced towards West Pier in the distance, and the

bright lights of Palace Pier behind it, and couldn't think of anywhere else he'd rather be. The coast had its own magic, even though some of the personal magic of this place had been taken away from him.

As he returned to his car, Scott's phone vibrated in his pocket. Yet again he attempted to get the swipe pattern right and failed several times. He succeeded and saw the text was from Cara.

Hope investigation is going well. Would be great to catch up again soon. x

Scott fired back his reply.

That would be nice. Speak soon.

Scott felt the familiar pangs of guilt creep up on him. His aching heart felt empty; his life felt broken and fractured. He sat there for a moment before reaching for his wallet and pulling out the small photos that had become so precious to him. They were photos of Tina, his wife, and their two-year-old daughter, Becky.

It had been three years since they were killed on Western Road by a hit-and-run driver. He'd seen it happen. They'd been trying to cross the road to meet him on the other side.

March 18 would always be etched into his psyche. The day his life changed forever. The force had rallied round him and given Scott compassionate leave. The driver had never been found, but the car was, burnt out on a dirt road near Devil's Dyke and the Brighton and Hove Golf Club.

He hoped the nightmares would diminish over time, and that the memories would become easier to cope with. But every day brought fresh pain.

Scott fought a daily battle with his conscience. He was riddled with guilt about moving on. Being in the company of another woman felt as though he was cheating on the memories of Tina.

28

It was seven a.m.; the sun was trying its hardest to creep up into the sky. The air felt decidedly chilly, and a cold mist clung to the coastline. The town was coming alive. A thin sparse line of cars snaked their way along Marine Parade, heading east towards Rottingdean.

The killer's next victim had been harder to track. The man lived for his nights, slept during the day and was rarely alone. This pattern had forced the killer to switch from night to day, leaving him vulnerable and exposed. He didn't care about being caught as long as he could cross these names off his list.

The killer watched from a distance, partly concealed by the undergrowth. This was one of the few occasions where his target was most vulnerable.

Today there were two cars in the open-air car park; one of those belonged to his target, the other to a middle-aged woman who walked her dog at six a.m. every day. He had watched her set off an hour ago in the direction of the fields behind Roedean School. She wouldn't be returning to her car for at least an hour. On average, her walks lasted ninety minutes to two hours.

The killer waited patiently for his target to return after taking his own dog for a walk. Crouching in the undergrowth had made his clothes damp from the morning dew, and he shivered. But his patience was rewarded when the man returned and opened the boot of his 4x4 to allow his Staffordshire to jump in.

The killer inched forward through the undergrowth, watching. He had become adept at moving unnoticed. He had chosen a quiet spot to attack, a place not overlooked by houses or the large school set back farther up the hill. He couldn't wait for another opportunity like this.

His victim moved around to the other side of the car out of sight, providing the ideal opportunity for him to approach the vehicle quickly. Loud music from the car stereo, the barking of his dog and the low drone of traffic snaking along the coast road cloaked his approach.

He withdrew his knife from beneath his hoodie, the steely blade catching the bright morning light.

His heart pounded; he could hear his own breath. Despite the chill, beads of sweat chased down the centre of his spine.

Each step in the gravel was gentle and careful as he came around the vehicle. The victim stood just in front of the open driver's door.

The killer lunged up from his crouched position. He needed all the height he could get, as his victim was built like an ox and well over six feet tall.

He thrust the knife down hard, the victim's waxy Barbour jacket offering little protection. A moment of panic hit him like a tidal wave when the blade didn't go in as far as he'd expected. Nevertheless, it was enough for the victim to fall to his knees, a throaty guttural scream breaking the silence.

The killer had to work quickly. The victim didn't collapse

in complete surrender, unlike the previous two; this one was proving a tough adversary.

You're making me work too hard, you fucker... You need to die.

The killer withdrew his knife before bringing it high above his head and driving it down once more with every ounce of energy he could.

The attack was frenzied and ferocious. The life drained from the victim.

Spent of energy, his muscles trembling, the killer stood exhausted, his eyes fixed wide. So lost in anger, he hadn't noticed his wet underwear and trousers. He grabbed the man's face and turned it to one side before pulling his victim's mouth open and stuffing three twenty-pound notes inside.

His focus was shattered by a piercing scream that came from somewhere behind him. Spinning on his knees, the lady dog walker stood to the rear of the vehicle, screaming hysterically. Her hands were clenched in fists either side of her head. Her face was sheer panic and terror. The Labrador by her side paced anxiously, staring up at its owner, unsure of how to react.

Shit, what is she doing here? She's early.

Gripped with new panic, his mind was spinning faster than a centrifuge.

What do I do?... No witnesses... Do I kill her, too?... Think, you idiot, think.

Killing her wasn't part of his plan; he had no axe to grind with her.

Why did you come back early?

He had only one option. Run. He ran right past her in the direction of Roedean Road, keen to put some distance between them.

His laboured breath drowned out her hysterical screams, and his mind flung into a cyclone of confusion.

Distance. Get away. The only words that made sense.

29

"Go away," Scott shouted as his mobile sprang into life from the bedroom.

He'd only jumped into the shower a few minutes earlier. When the phone stopped, he smiled and carried on lathering his body. Then it rang again; yet again he chose to ignore it. On the third occasion, he raced from the bathroom to answer it.

He grabbed his phone and saw that it was the station ringing. Scott knew it wouldn't be good news; they rarely called unless it was an emergency.

"Baker."

"Morning, sir, this is Sergeant Trillo, DCI Harvey asked me to get in contact with you immediately, as we've been called to an incident on the outskirts of town near Roedean School. There's been a fatality, a stabbing to be precise, and she requested that you attend."

"Okay, on my way. Where is it?"

"There's a small open-air car park on the corner of Marine Parade and Roedean Road. It's been cordoned off, and the DCI's already ordered SOCO over there."

"Can you get in touch with Trent and Wilson and ask them to meet me there?"

"Will do, sir."

Scott stood deep in thought, his eyes scanning the landscape outside his window. *Was this the work of our man?*

Just then his phone beeped. He looked at the screen to see it was a text message from the DCI. She asked him if he'd been called to the scene, to which he fired back,

Yes, on my way.

DCI Harvey's reply was almost instantaneous:

I'm en route now.

"Fuck, why is she heading out there?"

With that, Scott raced to his wardrobe and dressed whilst stumbling along the corridor and downstairs to the hallway. He almost fell out the front door in his search for his keys.

As he neared the location, traffic had slowed to watch the commotion. Scott took a left into Roedean Road and parked up. There was an ambulance on scene, several police cars, two white scientific service vans and an assortment of onlookers – the majority looked like dog walkers – being kept at bay by the police cordon.

The cordon was manned by a scene guard he recognised as PC Burgess. As he signed in and got kitted up in his forensic suit, Scott saw Abby and Mike pull up.

A white tent had been erected over the 4x4 and victim to keep prying eyes away and avoid distressing the locals. The scene that greeted Scott was horrific. Two scene-of-crime officers were taking detailed photos of the victim whilst a third SOCO combed the ground close to the vehicle. The ambulance had its back doors open, and two paramedics were tending to someone inside.

Scott approached the DCI, who was busy making notes. "What have we got, ma'am?"

"The victim was stabbed several times shortly after seven a.m. this morning. No visible signs of an altercation or defensive wounds for that matter. We've got a witness, a Mrs Janet Pembleton," she said, referring to her notes, "who saw the attacker. She's in the ambulance being treated for shock; she's given a very good description of the attacker. This could be the man we're looking for, Scott. Far too many similar characteristics to ignore, including the twenty-pound notes stuffed in the mouth," she finished, a sense of urgency clear in her voice.

"True, there are a lot of similarities: lone male, isolated spot, stabbed from behind," Scott said, looking at the surrounding area, "but the killer usually attacks at night."

Abby and Mike joined them.

The DCI gave Scott a pensive look. "I want you and the team to move on this quickly. It's only just happened. For all we know, the attacker could be close by. Flood the sodding area if you have to. I'm heading back to the office and will contact the chief super to keep him informed; you keep me updated hour by hour." She pointed at the ambulance. "If this is our man, he's fucked up this time."

When the DCI left, Scott turned to his team. "Mike, contact NPAS and find out if we can get air support to scan the local area, especially up there." He pointed to the area of scrubland and fields that lay to the left and beyond Roedean School. Scott hated all the abbreviations, but NPAS was far easier to say than the National Police Air Service.

Mike nodded before barking into his radio.

"Abby, organise uniform to go with you to check door to door up there." He pointed in the direction of Roedean Way. "The position of these houses means they have an elevated view over the car park and the surrounding scrubland. There's a possibility that a resident may have seen someone acting suspiciously."

Mike got off the radio. "Guv, we can't get air support for at least an hour. The nearest assistance is over in Worthing, and they're dealing with a failure to stop."

"Well, it was worth a shot, but I doubt our man would be stupid enough to be hiding up there." Scott scanned the surrounding area, looking for vantage points.

He instructed Mike to head over to Roedean School, the boarding school for girls that was in a prominent position at the top of the hill, to the right of the scene.

"Where are you headed, guv?" asked Mike.

"I'm going to speak to the witness."

30

Janet Pembleton sat in the back of the ambulance, draped in a standard red NHS blanket. She appeared to be in her mid-to-late forties, with light brown hair that was starting to go grey at the roots. She was dressed in a Barbour jacket, dark tight jeans and black riding boots.

She looked up as Scott stepped into the back of the ambulance. The familiar smell of hospital disinfectant greeted him. The paramedics stepped outside to give Scott some privacy.

He could see the terror in her bloodshot eyes. She had pulled the red blanket tight around her, forming a protective cocoon. She occasionally shivered, and Scott could tell that she was still trying to comprehend the horrific scene she'd witnessed.

"Mrs Pembleton, I'm Detective Inspector Scott Baker from Brighton CID." Scott presented his ID, which at first didn't register with her. Scott sat down opposite her and with a sympathetic, soft and measured tone that reflected the delicate situation, he asked, "May I ask you a few questions?"

Janet Pembleton stared at him through swollen red eyes for a few moments, as if deciding whether she was strong enough to cooperate or not.

Those few moments went on longer than Scott would have liked, but he knew the importance of giving the witness space and reassurance. The information that she had was vital to their investigation and could give him the breakthrough that he needed.

He'd often found that dealing with witnesses required a compassionate, yet firm stance. Officers were hardened to seeing the aftermath of violent crime; however, the average citizen was often left shocked, traumatised and unable to process what they had witnessed. Even though time was precious in the first few critical hours after a crime, it was often the allowance of time and space that helped to get results.

She finally gave the smallest of nods before looking away and down at the floor.

"I completely understand how you might be feeling after what you've witnessed. It would be really helpful if you could start from the beginning," he suggested, tilting his head to one side. "I know you've given your best account of what happened to my colleagues, and we really appreciate that. I'm the senior investigating officer in this case, so I'd also like to understand what happened here this morning."

There was a further silence, and Scott waited. Janet Pembleton's eyes shifted rapidly from left to right. Scott knew she was recalling the events in her mind and trying to make sense of them before explaining for a second time.

"Well… normally I take Benji out for about two hours, but this morning we cut short our walk because I had a coffee morning that I needed to attend, for my art class. The… the other… chap I see occasionally was parked to the left of my car, so it meant that as I returned from my walk, I had to go around his car to reach mine."

Janet paused for a moment, her mind clearly trying to organise the sequence of events.

"I walked around the back of his vehicle, and to begin with, I was looking out at the sea. It looked so beautiful, shimmering... but then something caught my attention to my left." She used her left hand to emphasise her point. "I... I looked down and saw a man kneeling over another chap who was face down. The man on the ground was covered in blood... covered... it was everywhere."

Her voice trembled; Scott noticed her hands were shaking a little.

"You're doing really well, Mrs Pembleton. Take your time," Scott reassured her gently.

"I just froze on the spot. I couldn't move. This kneeling man looked round at me. The look in his eyes. I'll never forget that. One second, they were full of anger, his face was twisted and snarling, and the next his eyes were wide and looked terrified. Like a schoolboy who'd been caught doing wrong..."

She trailed off and stared into space, lost in the thoughts.

Then she blinked and carried on. "He stood up and looked at me, and I saw this huge knife in his hand. It wasn't a normal type of knife. I remember seeing something similar in the *Rambo* films that I used to watch with my brothers. I just started to scream. He took a few steps towards me, and... I... I thought he was going to kill me." Janet began to cry, her shoulders shaking as she pulled the blanket in tighter around her body.

"Can you describe him to me, age, build, unusual features? Was he tall, short, well built? Anything would be helpful," Scott reassured her.

She thought hard, her eyes narrowing, her lips pursing.

"He was taller than me, and I'm five feet six, but I'd say he's shorter than you. I don't know, maybe about five feet nine or ten. He had a brown goatee beard. Mid-thirties. He had dark eyes, black jeans, a black hoodie and black shoes or trainers. I can't remember to be honest."

"And what happened next?"

"I... I just closed my eyes, thinking to myself, '*This is it*'." She closed her eyes as if reliving it again. "Then I just felt this rush of wind hit me, and the sound of footsteps followed. That's when I realised he'd run past me. I just froze. I don't think I opened my eyes for ages. I was so scared."

"Mrs Pembleton, you've been incredibly brave and so helpful. I can't thank you enough. I'll arrange for a uniformed officer to take you home and sit with you for as long as you need. I'll send one of my colleagues over from CID to take a full written statement, and we'd like to get an artist impression from you in the next hour or so. Thank you once again." Scott gave her an appreciative nod and left.

31

Cara had already been and gone by the time Scott had finished with the witness. Despite the situation, he had been looking forward to seeing her radiant smile once again. His mind flipped back to their quick drink. He almost mentally referred to it as a date, but it wasn't, was it? He wasn't sure.

Matt was on-site ensuring his team gathered and recorded the evidence thoroughly. On seeing Scott exit the ambulance, the SOCO beckoned him over by waving a clear evidence bag.

Scott made his way over, passing by discarded bottles, used condoms and general litter scattered towards the edges of this small car park.

"I've got an ID for your victim. Here's his wallet." Matt held up the clear evidence bag. "The victim is Peter Tomlins; his driving licence photo ID matches the person on the ground. He's certainly a big fella." Matt nodded at the mortuary team unloading a stretcher from the back of their black ambulance. "I feel sorry for those boys having to lift him."

Scott felt the hairs on the back of his neck stand up. The name had only come up a few times; however, it was the same name linked to the death of Stephen Wentworth.

Scott leant forward in his office chair to scan the information on his desk. As he read through the files, he began to build a clearer picture of the case from three years ago. Peter Tomlins had been the doorman for the Urban nightclub on the night that Stephen Wentworth died. Looking further down his charge sheet, Scott saw that several of Tomlin's previous convictions had been for assault on members of the public.

A bit heavy-handed, then, are you?

He was known in criminal circles as "Tommy", an enforcer of Dave Fraser's dirty work, and regularly trained out of the gym that Fraser owned.

What concerned Scott was that the case against Peter Tomlins had been dropped due to insufficient evidence and witness intimidation. The notes confirmed that CCTV footage from the club on the night in question was missing.

Scott flicked through the coroner's report that was attached to this case; he narrowed in on the concluding section. Scott read the last few sentences slowly.

"Post-mortem results concluded that Stephen had traces of cocaine and LSD in his bloodstream at the time of death. Stephen was knocked unconscious with one punch outside the Urban nightclub. It resulted in a bleed on the brain and his subsequent death."

Scott thumped the desk with his fist. He was certain that Stephen's death was now linked in some way to the three bodies in the morgue. Why? was his next question.

He stared at his notepad with the various directional

lines, hypotheses, and names, and muttered, "Why were they murdered, and how is Stephen connected to what is now a triple murder case?" He rubbed his temples in the hope of getting some clarity.

There were too many loose ends for Scott's liking. The cover-up, the twenty-pound notes, Stephen's death, and the supply chain for the drugs. It was whilst he was scanning the case file that something caught his attention.

He read the case notes on Dave Fraser a few times to make some sense of it... It stated that Dave Smith, the business partner of Lee Stubbins, had been murdered two years ago. Joe Stickle, an associate of Dave Fraser and Peter Tomlins, had been convicted of that murder.

Scott read the last line aloud. "... and is in Belmarsh prison serving seventeen years."

He pondered that for a minute as he added Joe Stickle to his map and drew a few extra lines to those already on it.

"This has to be a tit-for-tat thing."

He was pretty sure that Lee Stubbins was wrapped up in this. He had the most to gain from seeing Fraser and Tomlins out of the way. Why he would take out Stone was a different matter, and a question that Scott couldn't answer.

Scott pulled into the visitors' bay at the mortuary just before four p.m. Cara had emailed him earlier to say that she'd be performing the PM on Tomlins at three p.m. He got out of his car, hoping that he had missed most, if not all of it.

Cara was already stitching up Peter Tomlins when Scott knocked on the glass partition overlooking the inspection room. She greeted him with her familiar *come on in and join the party* wave.

Scott had never known someone to enjoy their job as much as her.

After getting prepped up in standard-issue green robes, he joined her and was greeted by the sounds of Radio One belting out a track he wasn't familiar with. It was coming from a radio sitting on a workbench close by. The presence of music softened the cold and clinical atmosphere he had felt in the room on his last visit.

"Hope you're not going to ask me to dance," he joked.

"Two left feet, Mr Baker?" Cara enquired, raising one eyebrow.

"You wish. I just don't want to show you up."

"Hope that's not a challenge?"

"*Moi*...? Never."

"Moving on to business again, your victim pissed off his killer. He was stabbed five times in close proximity." She lifted Tomlins's left shoulder and side up. "As you can see, he's also got bruising to the middle of his back."

Scott leant in to take a closer look before Cara laid the cadaver back down. The weight was clearly becoming too much for her to hold.

"Cause?"

"The bruising?"

He nodded.

"I'd say that he was stomped on a few times. I'm sure the attacks happened in quick succession."

"Why though?" Scott enquired.

"You're the detective, allegedly. I just give you the evidence. Having said that, this was a more violent and sustained attack than the previous ones, but it was more than likely carried out by the same instrument – your survival knife. On this occasion, it appears he really meted out some punishment... the attack was frenzied almost."

Scott said nothing. With his arms crossed and one hand supporting his chin, he stared at the body.

Cara continued, "As you can see, he's a big chap, with a very powerful torso, so it could be that it required more effort to disable him."

"That's quite possible, Cara."

"I've got hair fibres over there," she said, pointing to the workstation by her examination table. "I'll get them off now by courier to LGC in Oxford and rush them through. We should have preliminary results by the morning, but it will cost more if you want them to work on it through the night."

"Their forensics work twenty-four hours?"

"Yep."

"Do it, and I'll square it up with the DCI when I leave here. I need the results for my briefing tomorrow." Scott paused. "I owe you one, big time, Cara. Drinks on me next time."

"Make it dinner," she replied whilst holding his gaze.

"I'll text you," was the only reply he could manage.

32

His work was done; the killer felt neither remorse nor satisfaction. He seethed. *This isn't the way I wanted to feel.*

Saliva dripped from his mouth. He sat on the end of his bed, swaying gently back and forth as he clutched the black hoodie close to his chest. The cold emptiness of the room matched how he felt inside. He stared at the pictures that lay scattered around him on the floor.

The room was filled with the overpowering odour of stale urine, from the bundle of black clothes that lay in a messy heap in the corner of the room.

The curtains were drawn; just a few rays of light crept in from around the edges. The killer needed to be careful; he didn't want anyone peering in, even though he was on the first floor. He didn't want anyone to see the maps of Brighton he'd Blu-Tacked to the walls. Or the photos he'd taken of his victims as he stalked them, or the drawings he'd scrawled of each murder, done heavy-handedly with thick black pencils.

To anyone else they might think a ten-year-old child had

drawn them. Each one had a stick man lying on the floor, and another standing triumphantly over the victim, like a hunter over their latest kill in the African bush. The dimensions of the knife had been exaggerated in each picture to look as big as each of the characters.

Despite the savagery in the pictures, he'd still had time to draw flowers, cars and houses – the way children would draw them in preschool. If only life were that simple.

The chill that gripped him felt like he'd been plunged in to an ice bath. It had worked its way into every sinew of his being, like a parasite feeding off its host, getting stronger by the day whilst the host grew weaker.

The sadness he felt was buried deep within the pit of his stomach. Its tentacles had firmly secured themselves to him, like a pair of grappling hooks in crevices on a cliff face. Each penetrating spike held firm.

It wasn't supposed to end like this. He wanted to feel euphoric after taking the men out, that justice had somehow prevailed – an eye for an eye and all that. But he didn't, and it hadn't. None of it replaced what he'd lost.

As the killer stared into the emptiness, he questioned: *Where do I go now?*

He still carried too much hatred. There were others who needed to be held accountable. He had tried and failed to get to them; they were always surrounded by people in uniforms who drove cars with flashing blue lights.

His attention was drawn to the knife that lay on the floor, sparkling clean now, its recent history lost forever down the sink. He scrunched up his face, then began tugging aggressively at the small patches of eyebrow he still had left.

Using it would mean me having to get close.

The killer played out various scenarios in his head.

Maybe I should just wait here for them. They'll come and find me, and then I'll finish the job.

He liked that idea a lot. Excitement raced through his veins once again.

The killer fell back on the bed and closed his eyes, imagining exactly how he'd kill them when they found him.

33

Scott arrived early for work, keen to review any updates on the system. He'd delayed replying to Cara's text yesterday suggesting dinner, but had finally replied with a time after work, which she accepted.

The team were gathered in the briefing room by seven a.m. and watched Scott make a poor attempt at copying the spiderweb diagram from his notebook to the whiteboard.

It was met with the usual banter, the main culprit being Raj.

"Is it a plane? Is it a movie?" and, "How many syllables?"

Scott glanced over his shoulder to see Abby bite the rim of her coffee cup to stop herself from laughing, but her shaking shoulders gave her away.

He shrugged and turned to face Raj. "Fancy a stint back in uniform?"

That promptly wiped the pathetic grin from Raj's face and was met with even more laughter from the rest of the team.

"Mike and Abby, what are your updates from yesterday?" he asked.

Mike began. "I drew a blank at Roedean. I spoke to the principal and caretaker, they were naturally concerned about the pupils seeing us there, but I reassured them that there was no threat to their safety and that we'd be increasing patrols in the area for the next few days."

"I didn't get much further, guv," added Abby. "I spoke to the residents. Most were in, and I left messages for those not answering. One resident has her artist studio set up in a front room that takes advantage of the sea views. She saw the 4x4 there about six thirty a.m. when she got up, but she wasn't back at the window till about seven forty-five a.m. At that point she saw the police presence."

Scott blew out a long breath. "This is a nightmare."

As if mysteriously sensing the bind Scott was in, the door opened, and DCI Harvey walked in.

"Thought I'd see what updates we have after yesterday, Scott."

To add to the pressure, the DCI stood by the door and leant back on the wall, her arms crossed.

Could this day start off any worse?

"Yes, ma'am. Thanks for authorising the hair fibre analysis rush job. The results came through about an hour ago. The fibre matches those found on the other two victims, so we're looking for the same person. This person has systematically hunted down and killed three men who were known to each other. So that's one connection. I'm certain Lee Stubbins has something to do with it because he wanted the second victim, Dave Fraser, out of the way to acquire the distribution channels, so he could have ordered his hit and one on his business partner, who was killed by an associate known to these men."

The DCI nodded in approval.

Scott continued to his team, "We also need to look closely at the Stephen Wentworth link, because Pete Tomlins was charged as a result of his death. I started on Stephen's background yesterday, and Sian did Stubbins's."

"Makes sense, guv," said Raj. "You reckon it's a revenge thing?"

"Possibly, it's worth keeping that motive on the table. I did some research last night, and it appears Stephen's parents split up long ago. I've not found out where his mum is. Can you investigate that, Mike?"

Mike nodded.

"Anything else?" Scott asked his team.

Sian raised her pen. "Stone's contact list threw up frequent calls to both Vicky and Dave Fraser, and the others were club-related contacts."

Abby added, "I tugged on a few collars… the dealers and users we know, and as Mike found out too, if you wanted some *gear*, the Phoenix and Urban were the places to go. Interestingly, a few dealers had been visited by Tomlins in the past whenever they were slow on payments."

Scott nodded. "We've got two things going on here. We've got a triple murder case, and we've got a case from three years ago tied into it. Whoever was there three years ago was also present in some way at all three murders in the past ten days. Raj, I want you to go through the files again and see if we've missed anything, and get me an update on the artist impression from our witness. We need that to go out in a press appeal today." He nodded at DCI Harvey. "Square it with ma'am when you get it and then pass it to the press officer."

Scott looked around at the team. "Any other business?" His request was met with a collective shake of heads. "Let's get to work, then."

The DCI left the room.

He gathered his notes and files into a bundle. "Abby, you and I are going to talk to Stephen's father. I found his last known address in Shoreham, so let's pay a visit."

"Does the job ever get too much for you, guv?" Abby questioned as she looked out to sea.

As Scott drove along the seafront to Shoreham, he didn't need to look at her to know where her focus was.

It was a question that had crossed his mind on many an occasion. Certainly the last few years had been a challenge, and the job regularly tested him as an officer. The more senior in the ranks he rose, the greater the pressure and the more accountability he inherited. The personal trials he'd faced had made him question life in general.

But that wasn't something he felt comfortable discussing with Abby, even though he considered her a good friend. He liked her; she was open, honest and a real grafter. What you saw was what you got with her. She carried similar traits and beliefs to him and would go far in her career.

Scott tried to answer in the best way he could without sounding negative or judgemental. "It can. I guess two days are never the same, so it can be difficult to balance the highs with the lows."

Abby blew out a long, slow breath in frustration.

"Why, what's up?" Scott asked.

"Nothing, guv." She paused, and Scott felt there was more to come. "I guess I find it hard to keep motivated some days. I'm rushing around like a blue-arsed fly. We hardly do a nine-to-five, and sometimes I wish we did."

Scott knew the feeling well.

"I hardly get any time to myself," she continued. "When I get home, there's the house to clean, the kids to sort out, homework, ironing... and the list goes on. By the time that's done, all I'm good for is collapsing in bed."

"You must get out sometimes, surely."

Abby ran her hand through her hair and laughed. "Social life? What's that?"

As her senior officer, Scott had a responsibility to monitor the welfare of his staff. He endeavoured to support his team in any way he could. He felt personally responsible for them. If they did well, he was the first in line to praise them. When they fell, he was their safety net.

"You thought about reducing your hours, or job sharing?" he suggested.

"If I did that, guv, I wouldn't be able to afford my mortgage or pay for the kids' clubs."

"Well, I know we're pushed on this case, but once we're done, take a few days off. You're owed some anyway from last month when we worked on that serial burglary case. You put in more hours than anyone else."

Abby nodded but didn't respond.

Her mood worried him. This was something he'd need to take up with her once the case was over. Abby was a great asset, and Scott would do his best to support her.

Good experienced officers were hard to come by. He wasn't willing to lose her.

34

Park Avenue was a mixture of houses and bungalows. The property they were interested in was a small, unkempt bungalow that lacked the pride other properties in the street showed off. It was a well-kept quiet street, with small front gardens surrounded by privacy shrubs or dwarf walls. Scott imagined that most of the residents were retirees who had opted for single-storey living after they downsized.

The door was answered by a gaunt, thin-framed man. He had brown hair that was fading to grey, his jeans looked a size too big, and his shirt hung loose.

"Mr Adams? Mr Jim Adams?" Scott enquired.

The man nodded.

"I'm Detective Inspector Baker, and this is Detective Sergeant Trent from Brighton CID. May we come in and ask you a few questions?"

Scott held up his warrant card. Jim Adams glanced at it. He nodded for them to come in and walked away.

Scott closed the front door, and he and Abby followed

him into the lounge. It was surprisingly clean and tidy, but not modern by any stretch of the imagination. The officers sat on the worn burgundy leather sofa, whilst Adams sat opposite them in a matching armchair.

"What can I do for you?" he asked.

Scott noticed the yellow staining on Adam's remaining teeth. He estimated that he'd lost at least a quarter of them.

Abby was poised with her notebook and pen.

Scott started. "We wanted to talk to you about your son, Stephen."

Adams hunched up and pinned his hands between his legs. He shot a confused looked at Scott and Abby, then pursed his lips and nodded. "That's a name I've not heard for many years."

Abby swapped a look with Scott before he continued, "Not heard, Mr Adams? When's the last time you saw Stephen?"

"I've never seen him, Detective Inspector. His mother ran away before she had the kid. God knows what he's up to, where he is, or even what he looks like." Adams circled his left hand.

This wasn't turning out the way Scott had expected. He had hoped to ask Jim Adams questions about his son. Instead, he was about to pass on the news that his son had been killed three years ago.

Scott cleared his throat. "Mr Adams, I'm sorry to inform you that your son was killed three years ago in Brighton."

Adams lifted his head in surprise, a look of unknowing in his eyes. "In Brighton? He was down here?"

Scott wasn't sure what to make of his reaction. Adams seemed more unfazed and surprised than anything else.

"What happened to him?"

"He was attacked outside a nightclub and died from head injuries he sustained."

Adams nodded and said nothing.

It was becoming apparent that Adams wasn't going to be able to shed much light on Stephen's case or his background. Scott tried a different tack.

"What happened to his mother?"

Adams rubbed the stubble on his cheek. "Not long after getting knocked up, she walked out on me and moved back to Reading, where her parents lived. She told me she couldn't do this any longer, that it was too much. She upped and left. Bags and all."

Adams stopped and looked down at the carpet. A short pause silenced the room. "That was that... I didn't hear from her until after she'd had the boy."

"Why did she leave?" Abby pressed the point.

Adams looked a bit sheepish before continuing, "Well, you see, we were just having fun back then. We'd been seeing each other for a year or so, maybe longer. It was an accident, really. We were off our faces most of the time. She liked the puff and charlie, and I liked the red stripe. Too much of both as you can tell." He pointed at his remaining teeth. "I told her we could get rid of it, but by then she was freaking out, angry, snorting line after line."

"Did you try to make her stay?" Abby asked.

"Nah, didn't see the point. I wasn't looking to be a dad; she didn't want to hang around..." He trailed off and shrugged.

"What was her name?" asked Scott.

"Jackie... Jackie Taylor."

"Date of birth?"

"That's easy; it was 1 August. Can't remember the year, but I think she was about nineteen when I met her."

Scott concluded the visit, knowing he'd gained as much as he could.

"Mr Adams, you've been very helpful. Thank you for your time."

As they walked back to the car, Abby paused by the passenger door and leant across the roof. "Wonder why he never tried to track her down?"

"I guess if he didn't want a child and considered it a *mistake*," said Scott, "then he might feel that way?"

35

Scott darted back to the station to approve the e-fit of the suspect based on the eyewitness report. It would go out that evening to the *Argus*, *Brighton & Hove Independent* and BBC Sussex websites. Though it would be two days before the e-fit and press appeal would go to print, Scott hoped to leverage the power of online media to gain quicker exposure.

Encouragingly, the image offered a detailed description, thanks to Mrs Pembleton. It had been their first major sighting, and often eyewitness accounts in many cases had been key to getting results.

SCOTT ARRIVED at the Chilli Pickle, a popular and trendy Indian restaurant, a few minutes before seven thirty p.m. He was munching on some poppadoms when he saw Cara approaching.

She was dressed in tight, dark blue jeans, a white

crocheted top and navy heels, her coat slung over her arm. The whole outfit accentuated her toned figure. His jaw dropped.

"You seem to be having difficulty closing your mouth," she teased.

"Erm, yes... sorry. I mean no." Scott struggled to find the right words. He stood and kissed her on the cheek. "You look fab."

Scott cursed himself. *You idiot, is that the best you could come up with... fab of all words?*

She laughed. "So do you, Detective."

Scott glanced at his suit, now crumpled having sat in the car. "Personally, I would have come in jeans too, but I came straight from work, so didn't have time to change. I feel a bit overdressed to be honest." He pulled at the lapels on his jacket.

Cars waved her hand and sat down. "Don't be daft; you look smart and stylish. I like the way you dress. Formal yet fashionable. I remember going out with a guy a long time ago who wore trainers with trousers. He looked like such a prat." She winced as she described him. "He actually thought he looked really cool."

"If you think that's bad, I think the DCI wins the award for least coordinated person. She wears these big oversized cardigans that hang down to her knees. Bless her, she's short enough, and they look like printed parachutes on her."

Cara rocked back in her chair, trying to muffle a roar of laughter.

They ordered drinks and shared a few small plates of Persian biryani, masala dosa and a tandoori chicken platter. They greeted the food with approving groans of pleasure and tucked into the shared dishes.

Scott loved the ease with which the conversation flowed

between them. He could be himself and relax without fear of judgement. He wasn't sure if that was down to chemistry or because Cara was so bubbly and sociable. It was probably a bit of both.

The atmosphere helped too, with its bright cultural colours and decorative fixtures. The excited hum from other diners and the smell of traditional Asian spices filled the air and added to the ambience.

The conversation soon moved to the case. Cara asked a lot of questions and appeared genuinely interested in its progress. In fact, Scott feared she'd spoken too much and that he hadn't asked her much in return.

Scott told her about the developments and the e-fit construction, as well as his expectation that it should yield some results. He took a quick swig of beer and was about to carry on when Cara interrupted him.

"You know the twenty-pound-notes thingy?" she said whilst moving food around her plate. "I've got a theory, but promise you won't laugh?"

"Oh really, I'm intrigued, Detective Hall," Scott jested with a raised eyebrow.

"Promise? Or the chutney sauce goes over you." She threatened in a playful tone, waving a small metal dish in front of him.

"Okay, okay, deal," he conceded, holding his hands up in surrender.

"Well, as you know, I'm interested in all things morbid, and I've got an idea."

Scott watched, captivated by her animated style as she waved her hands around.

"I've always been interested in the Mafia, or the Cosa Nostra as they like to refer to themselves across the pond. I was thinking about your case this morning, and the money-in-the-mouth thing. Then I remembered reading that the Mafia used to punish their own in a certain way based on the crime they had committed. So if a guy had committed a sex crime or adultery, they'd cut off his dick."

Scott nearly choked on his food as his eyes grew wide.

"Now here's the interesting thing, Scott. People who had stolen or embezzled or had become too fixated on money would have money stuffed in their mouths after being killed." Cara paused for a moment to push that point home before continuing, "The money in the mouth reflected greed." She pointed in Scott's direction to reinforce the word and nodded. "Greed."

Scott stayed quiet as he thought about Cara's theory.

Cara raised her eyebrows. "Well?" She leant over the table and, with a circling motion of her hand, pushed for a reaction. "Credible or stupid?"

"Hmm," was the only response he gave. His gaze drifted off in no particular direction, to continue crunching through her theory.

"Is that it?" she asked, startled by his lack of enthusiasm. She must have hoped for at least an agreement, or that he would thank her for giving him a bit more food for thought.

She sighed, sounding deflated after initially being so excited to tell him.

Scott's attention drifted back to the table. He stared at Cara for what felt an eternity, but in reality, was just a second or two.

She frowned at him. "Why are you looking at me like that? Have I got food on my face?" Cara lifted a napkin.

"You know, you may have hit on something there. We could have a motive, it's certainly plausible."

The smile returned to her face. "See, not just a pretty face."

He had to agree; brains and beauty wrapped up in a delightful package.

Scott and Cara ended their night sharing a kulfi and gulab jamun for dessert; the cold of the ice cream and the sweetness of the jamun refreshed their palates. But Cara found the jamun too sweet for her liking, leaving a happy Scott to mop up both desserts.

36

The cold air bit into their skin the moment they stepped outside. Their clothes offered little protection in this weather. Cara stamped her feet to keep warm.

"We should have stayed in there," said Scott as he rubbed his hands together.

"I had a lovely evening, Scott. You're really easy to get on with. The next one's on me, okay?"

He grinned. "Deal... It was good fun."

"Why are you grinning? What's so funny?" She laughed a little.

"Don't know, just had a cracking night, I guess. I'm heading back to Regency Square. Where are you parked?"

"I got a cab here, so I'll call for one now."

Scott didn't want the evening to end; the thought of going back to an empty house didn't fill him with excitement. He knew he had to do some work, but it could wait till later. Sensing Cara wasn't wishing for the evening to end either, and both hesitant to say as much, Scott broke the silence.

"Well, do you fancy walking back to the car park with me,

and I'll drop you home? I know it's a bit chilly, but if we walk fast…" He left the suggestion hanging.

"In these bloody things, are you for real?" She laughed, lifting her foot off the ground to show him her four-inch heels.

"Fair point. Well, then a slow walk to the car park, and if your feet hurt, I'll give you a piggyback," he said, teasing her with a quick wink.

"Hey, listen, you try to carry me, and you'll be in A & E with a slipped disc by the end of tonight."

Scott stuck out his elbow. Cara fed her arm through his, and they headed into town to cut through on to West Street and towards the seafront.

They said nothing for most of their walk, just enjoying the vibrancy of the town and the sound of dozens of conversations erupting from the pubs, restaurants and bars they passed.

Cara's heels tapped quickly over the pavement, creating a hypnotic beat as they walked along the promenade past the Grand Hotel, its illuminated, imposing white frontage adding to the majestic and opulent feel of the property.

"Have you ever wondered why you do your job?" she asked.

He sighed. "Every day."

"Is that a good or bad thing?"

"Probably both to be honest. It can sometimes feel like a thankless task."

"What do you mean?" Her questioning eyes fixed on him.

Scott pulled up the collar on his jacket to shield himself from the cold night air that was whipping around them. "Well, you join the force to make a difference, but sometimes you feel like you can never win."

"Go on." Cara nudged him.

"The public are quick to criticise when crimes go

unsolved but full of praise when you come to their rescue. Then the support you hope to get from within the force doesn't always materialise. The bosses want results on the one hand but take away your resources and cut budgets on the other."

"I see what you mean about thankless," she said consolingly as she gave his arm a reassuring squeeze.

"To add to that, you have officers who are completely stressed. I end up doing at least one welfare home visit every few weeks to officers signed off with stress, depression, drinking problems – and that's just the tip of the iceberg." Scott blew out air through his lips.

"Well, if things ever get too much for you, you do know you can talk to me anytime?" She nudged him again with her shoulder.

Scott looked at her with an appreciative smile. He knew there was sincerity in her offer, and it was gladly welcomed, even if he didn't tell her.

37

The following morning, Scott strode through the station with purpose, his case file in one hand, the remains of his double espresso in the other, and a large, smug grin. He needed the caffeine to kick in and charge through his body. His eyes were heavy, the skin around his eyelids fatigued. He worked hard to fight the urge to find a dark corner in the office, curl up and fall asleep for a few hours.

After dropping Cara off, he'd worked late into the night researching the suggestion that Cara had come up with. At the time he'd partially dismissed her idea, putting it down to her wonderful and often weird, creative imagination. However, after some time looking at its plausibility, he had to admit that it warranted further exploration.

His exploration had paid off.

As he pushed through the doors of CID, he felt renewed energy spurring him on. He called out to no one in particular, "Drop whatever you're doing and get your arses in the briefing room. We've got a new line of enquiry."

Mike and Abby looked up as Scott passed their desk. He

disappeared through the double doors at the end of the office that led up to the briefing room. He pictured them exchanging a curious glance and Abby raising her brows to suggest *here we go again*.

The team entered the room, all exchanging curious glances with Scott before grabbing a seat. Raj was still munching on his chocolate croissant whilst gingerly balancing his mug of tea on his notepad.

"Where's mine, you fat pig?" Mike demanded, looking at the warm croissant.

"Erm, pot and kettle and black spring to mind," Raj retaliated with a wink.

Mike glared at him, and for a moment their eyes had a gladiatorial battle.

"Ladies, when you've finished having your handbag fight, if you could pay attention," Scott said.

He waited until he had everyone's attention.

"As you know, this issue around the money in the mouth has been bugging me since the start of the case. Dealing with a killer who's taken down three victims in under two weeks is bad enough, but the significance of the three twenty-pound notes in each of the victim's mouths is integral to the motive."

Scott paced the length of the briefing room, working through his thoughts as he talked.

"I had a chat with Cara yesterday and found out that stuffing money in the mouth of the victim was something that the Mafia used to do to demonstrate that the victim had been greedy..." He paused before continuing, "There's a strong likelihood that the motive behind these crimes is to do with greed."

"Are you suggesting our killer believes the victims were greedy?" interrupted Abby.

"Yes, Abby." Scott paused as he reflected. "It doesn't take us any further down the line of identifying who the killer is, but it could suggest the driving force behind his killing spree."

"And do you think Stubbins is still complicit in these murders?" asked Abby.

Scott turned to her. "What's on your mind?"

"Well, I can see the tenuous link between the victims, Stubbins, and the whole thing being about greed..." She paused and tapped her pen on her notepad. "And if we can find the evidence to link Stubbins into these, then that's a great result. However, it doesn't help with solving why the same DNA hair fibre profile was found on each of the victims." She shook her head. "I don't get that bit."

"I know what you mean," Scott continued. "We had the e-fit go out last night, so, Raj, I want you to help Mike man the phones this morning. Anything of interest that comes through, let me know straight away."

The officers nodded their agreement, though Scott could tell from Raj's face that he was hoping to get stuck into something a bit meatier than handling calls from members of the public.

"Abby, I want you to organise a couple of tickets for us to go back and see Stubbins. I'll get the DCI to contact the governor at Pentonville so we can do a search of his cell whilst we're there. If he's arranged the hits, then he must have some way of communicating with the outside. He's either used a phone or passed his instructions through a visitor, so we need to check the visitor log."

38

Their second visit to Pentonville was in marked contrast to the first. The prison governor and his deputy met them in reception and weren't pleased to have the request sprung on them at the very last minute. The governor expressed in no uncertain terms that he would be having words with the chief constable. Scott shrugged it off, knowing it wasn't his battle to fight; there was a triple murder investigation at stake; he was happy to leave the political one-upmanship to others.

Stubbins was equally annoyed and started spouting off about breaches to his human rights as he was led away from his cell by prison officers.

The deputy governor accompanied them and stood in the doorway of the cell after Scott and Abby entered.

Scott was greeted with the overpowering smell of human excrement that sent waves of nausea rippling through his stomach. Abby gagged, and they both shot a glance at the metal toilet in the corner of the cell, partially shielded by a low wall that separated it from the combined sleeping and living quarters.

Though Scott had little sympathy for inmates, he never understood how prisoners coped with degrading conditions that allowed the most intimate of habits to be on full display for others to see.

"Stubbins left us a calling card." Abby tried not to retch as she buried her nose and mouth into the crook of her elbow.

Prison cells were often small and cramped, holding two or three inmates per cell. This meant that Scott and Abby had to tread carefully, as they had not been given permission to search the space or the possessions of the other inmate.

Whilst Abby went through Stubbins's small bookshelf, Scott patted down Stubbins's pillow and bedding, looking for any signs of a mobile phone or other communication device. He knew Stubbins was too clever to leave a phone lying around but lifted the mattress to peer underneath, on the off chance there was one stashed beneath it. Scott had to accept that Stubbins could have concealed items in the belongings of the other inmate, knowing they were off-limits.

The search revealed nothing, as Scott had anticipated, but secretly, he wanted to send a clear message to Stubbins to let him know that he was still in the frame and on their radar. The deputy governor sneered and taunted them about the waste of police resources.

"We could have done this for you, and frankly, babysitting you is a waste of my time."

That comment riled Scott.

Frustrated over the lack of cooperation, Scott strode over to the deputy governor, who was leaning against the door frame looking smug, his arms folded. Scott's six-foot frame towered over the short man. They were almost touching toe to toe.

Scott could smell the man's stale breath and a strong pungent hint of onion, no doubt from eating a packet of cheese and onion crisps – or several, judging by the man's round face and double chin. He wore an ill-fitting grey suit, with his leather belt straining to stop his beer belly from spilling out over the top.

Scott locked his steely eyes with the man. The deputy governor's breath caught in his throat as he shuffled on the spot. Pinned to the door frame, he had little room to manoeuvre.

"We are supposed to be on the same side," Scott growled. "If you impede my search in any way, I'll make sure you're back in uniform and patrolling the prison's corridors before your tubby arse has a chance to sit down."

He heard Abby stifle a laugh. To defuse the situation, most likely, she said, "We're done here, Deputy Governor. We would like to look at the visitors' log, if that's okay with you?"

The deputy governor swallowed hard, a glisten of perspiration breaking out on his balding head. What little hair he had on his head had been parted and combed in a vain attempt to disguise his receding hairline.

He escorted the officers in silence to the front reception, unlocking doors to allow them to pass before locking them again afterwards. He let them out into the main reception area without saying a word, like a schoolboy chastised.

As Scott peered through the reinforced glass panel in the door, he saw the deputy governor disappear back into the prison, reach for his mobile phone and drop it in the process.

Scott wondered whom he needed to call so urgently.

"Prat."

Scott fumed under his breath as he joined Abby, who was already talking to the prison guard behind the reception desk. Scott felt like a gooseberry as the officer tried to chat Abby up, with Abby enjoying the attention. Abby's cheeks flushed when she noticed Scott teasing her with a smile and wink.

The officer tapped away on a keyboard, and Abby waited

patiently. The printer by the screen whirred into life, then spewed out a printout. The guard pulled it off and passed it to Abby before heading off to get the CCTV footage for those visits.

Scott smiled at her.

"What?" she said accusingly.

"Shall I get you a quiet table in the corner so you can get to know him better?"

His suggestion was answered with a gentle kick, causing Scott to wince.

They both scanned through the entries – all five of them – and then exchanged an encouraging glance.

"Seems he's not that popular, guv." Abby laughed. She pointed at one name. "Lewis Samuels, that name hasn't popped up in our investigations."

"No, it hasn't, but I've got a hunch," Scott said, tapping one finger on his temple.

"Another one of your hunches, guv?"

The prison guard returned and showed them to a separate room where he loaded up the five visits on a large bank of monitors fixed to the wall. As they peered over his shoulder, Scott saw the grainy image of the same man arriving on all five occasions. The man looked like he was in his mid-thirties, broad shoulders that were hidden beneath a black baggy jacket. He was smartly dressed, but not enough to draw unnecessary attention to himself.

Abby took a closer look, leaning more over the prison guard's shoulder. "He does look familiar, guv."

"That's because he is. In his mugshot he hasn't got the long hair tied in a ponytail that he has now, nor does he have a goatee beard."

The penny dropped; she shot Scott a glance. "Seriously is that him?"

"I'm pretty certain it is."

Abby checked the scans of the driving licence and proof of address that each prison visitor needed to provide. They were all in the name of Lewis Samuels. "These are fake, guv."

"Well, they have the resources and connections to get plausible fakes made up. How else do you think they travel overseas when on the run or when trying to stay under the police radar?"

Abby tutted with frustration.

Scott added. "I think we've found our messenger or killer... Or both."

39

Raj and Mike spent most of the previous day fielding the steady stream of calls that had resulted from the e-fit and press release. The level of public interest had been healthy, as Scott had expected. The third murder had taken place a few days ago. It was still fresh, and more importantly, members of the public were concerned about a murderer on the loose.

Raj was pissed off about the volume of callers asking irrelevant questions, such as why there wasn't a stronger police presence on the streets to capture the killer, could they have more officers on the beat, and more effort was needed to address the parking problems in residential streets.

"I sound like a parrot," Raj moaned.

Mike shrugged it off, knowing it was a necessary and vital task. "The public are our second set of eyes on the street, mate," he reasoned, even though a part of him likely agreed with Raj.

Scott watched his team work.

Mike's army days had taught him not to pussyfoot around. "If you want something, then fucking go and get it," his troop sergeant used to bark in his ears. "Hunt or be hunted, the hunter is not the fucking hunted," were doctrines his sergeant apparently drilled into every squaddie during training.

Though it was ethically wrong and would result in a disciplinary, Mike would rather round up all the lowlifes in Brighton and rough them up a bit until the undesirables of Brighton gave up one of their own.

In Scott's opinion, the appeal had received good coverage last night, thanks to the efforts of the press office. All major news channels both national and local had dedicated a few minutes of airtime to cover the series of murders that had taken place in the last two weeks.

The appeal had highlighted the eyewitness e-fit, the locations, together with suitable comments from the deputy chief constable of Sussex Police. It was the usual PR stuff about the need to maintain vigilance, report any suspicious activity and that all the resources available to Sussex Police were being deployed. The DCC went to great lengths to stress the primary focus of the force was the safety of the public.

The news piece ended with the offer that information could be passed on anonymously to Crimestoppers on the relevant number.

WITH THE DOOR CLOSED, Scott savoured his black coffee whilst reviewing the summary of calls that Raj and Mike had vetted. Nothing stood out. The odd person had mentioned seeing someone resembling the suspect in a pub, or in passing. However, nothing could be corroborated or warranted further investigation.

His thinking time was interrupted with a knock on his door, followed by the DCI breezing in.

With bloodshot eyes, she looked tired in her face.

She's either had a skinful last night or very little sleep.

"Bloody good coverage last night," she remarked.

If he closed his eyes, her gravelly voice would have sounded like a sexy Sharon Stone or Kathleen Turner, but reality didn't quite match up with fantasy.

The DCI took in a huge lungful of air before letting out a mucous-filled cough that repulsed Scott. She rubbed her chest in an attempt to soothe it, whilst taking a sip of coffee from her favourite mug emblazoned with the logo *I'm the BOSS*.

"Any valuable leads so far?"

Scott wished she would take her cough, mucous and her stale cigarette breath out on to the main floor. He'd much rather she contaminated the air out there than spread her germs inside his small office.

"Nothing yet, ma'am, but I'm confident that we'll get a breakthrough with this appeal." He rolled a pen through his fingers.

Scott had a plan of some sorts. The press release and appeal would be the catalyst for it. For the time being, he would keep it close to his chest in case his hunch was wrong.

"The chief super's getting pressure, so we need more, Scott." The DCI left.

Harvey's parting words were few, but the intention behind them wasn't lost on him. She wanted results, and she wanted them now.

Scott trawled through his workbook again, reviewing his notes, challenging his own assumptions and figuring out his next step. There were loose ends that still didn't add up.

They had a clear e-fit of the killer, but they didn't match the stills taken of Stubbins's visitor. Was there more than one killer? A pair working together? Did this have a faint whiff of sanctioned hits by another criminal gang? They had Stubbins in the frame, and they had a motive for the money. Now he just needed to get the last few pieces that would bind it all together, and one of those was the connection with Stephen's hair fibres found on each victim.

He stared at his drawings, his eyes flicking from point to point, the cogs of his brain digesting the information. The pictures of the crime scenes flashed in his mind, like he was watching a series of stills on a movie screen. The post-mortem visits, Cara's input, the events and sequences as they happened over the past two weeks... he processed and reviewed them in a matter of seconds.

Scott was pulled from his thoughts when Mike hammered on the door.

Scott waved him in. "This'd better be good, Mike."

"It is, guv. We've had three sightings of a person resembling the e-fit."

"Where?"

"Shoreham."

This was more than a coincidence. "Get me the details quickly."

Scott spun round in his chair and started searching on Google and joint operational databases; he needed more background on Stephen Wentworth and his parents. Very little was known about that family.

If you could call it a family.

It saddened him knowing how many children were brought into the world by dysfunctional families or as accidents after one too many drunken flings.

The gift of life was precious in his eyes. Having lost a child, it tugged on his heartstrings even more. He'd lost count of the number of times he'd seen a young child playing or walking with their mum and been filled with a deep pain that only a parent who'd lost a child could relate to.

He blinked hard to clear the tears that blurred his view of

the screen. There would be other times when he could sit and be alone with the grief that followed him like a dark shadow. For now, he needed to focus and prove his suspicions right.

When he found the right website, the first thing he entered was *Jackie Taylor, March 1.*

40

The reports of the same person being sighted in Shoreham were sufficient for Scott to send Mike and Abby to investigate further. If the sightings were confirmed, it would warrant Scott asking DI Harvey to assign more resources to the area for detailed house-to-house enquiries.

Scott furiously scanned multiple records, lines of entry and columns. Jackie Taylor was a popular name, which didn't surprise Scott, but neither did it please him. It made it harder to narrow down his search.

The records pulled up entries for both deaths and births. He leant closer to the screen, the information powerful enough to suck him in like a vortex. His mind was a mixture of confusion and clarity, and he found it hard to interpret the evidence being thrown back at him.

His heartbeat quickened, his breath came short and rapid, and the hairs on the back of his neck stood up. His clammy left hand stuck to the paper pad he was resting it on; his right hand, equally clammy, squealed across the desk as he moved the mouse around quickly, from one screen to another.

Raj burst through the door, not pausing to knock and certainly not learning from his recent chastisement. Luckily for him, Scott was too swept up in the evidence in front of him to care. Raj's information would only add more fuel to the fire, as he was about to find out.

Scott reluctantly pulled his attention away to glance at Raj, who was trying to compose himself. It looked comical to say the least as the officer stood there, a notepad in one hand and half-eaten Bakewell tart slice in the other. As all the officers had become accustomed to, where there was Raj, there would be food.

Flicking between his monitor and Raj, he circled his left hand in the air to hurry Raj along.

"Guv, I've just had a call from a B & B owner in Shoreham. It's the White Lawns in Buckingham Road. He's certain that he has a guest with an uncanny resemblance to our man. He said he's hardly seen the man. He's in his room all day and goes out at night. He can hear the door opening at all hours of the early morning. And he's been told not to clean the room or enter."

Scott wasn't sure if it was the eyewitness account that rocked him the most or what he'd just read on-screen. But he knew the case had reached a tipping point.

He stood up and reached for his jacket, shouting at Raj, "Get Abby and Mike over there now. Tell them to meet us there, but under no circumstances should they go in until we arrive. Tell them to park up at a discreet distance and watch the place, get some uniform on standby in a neighbouring road."

"What, me too, guv?" Raj said in surprise, caught off guard by Scott's sudden frenetic reaction.

"Yes, you plank, unless you want to stay and man the phones?"

Raj didn't need asking twice. He stuffed the remnants of the tart in his mouth, grabbed his jacket on the way out and was already on his radio passing on the instructions.

Scott headed out the door. "Sian, you too."

Sian left the research she was doing and bolted for the door too, grabbing her handbag and radio in one deft swipe.

Scott left the office and flew down the steps, taking them two at a time.

41

The White Lawns B & B was situated on a quiet, tree-lined street in Shoreham. The houses had large, detached frontages, with the occasional semi-detached des res dotted in between them.

The address they were interested in belonged to a period property. From the outside it was apparent that at one time it had been a semi-detached house. In more recent times, it had been merged with its adjoining twin. It now presented as a larger detached property that better suited its change of use from a domestic dwelling to a small commercial bed and breakfast offering.

Having parked about fifty yards up the road, Mike and Abby reported no movement or sightings. Scott requested they remain there for the time being.

"Raj, considering you've spoken to the owner, I want you to go in first and, if there's no one around, ask him discreetly to confirm again that one of his guests matches the e-fit."

Raj headed off. Moments later, he appeared from the front door and pulled out his phone.

A few seconds later, Scott's phoned pinged. Glancing at

the screen, he saw the message was from Raj telling him that their suspect went out earlier and hadn't returned.

Scott told Mike to watch the front, and Abby to monitor the rear of the property in case the man returned.

The property had a sweeping entrance and exit to allow guests to drive in and unload in safety before parking to the side of the property, where there was guest parking for up to four cars.

Scott met Raj, who was standing with the proprietor. The man was of average height and build, mousey brown hair, combed and parted on the left, and wearing a plain, light blue shirt and cream chinos. If Scott had to describe a nondescript person, this man would be it.

Scott produced his warrant card. "I'm Detective Inspector Baker. I understand you have a guest here matching the description of a person we're interested in?"

The man nodded nervously. "Yes, I'm Barry Burgess." Unsure what else to say, he extended his hand towards Scott, then stopped. "Will this take long?"

He had a jittery intensity about him; his shoulders were hunched, he was wringing his hands, and his feet shuffled on the spot.

"Having the police turn up isn't great for PR, if you know what I mean," he mumbled as he glanced over Scott's shoulder towards the street, probably concerned about the curtain twitchers.

"Mr Burgess, let me remind you that I'm investigating a triple murder case here. I don't care what your neighbours think. I'll happily leave the suspect in your hands to deal with."

Burgess, shocked and frightened at the prospect of having a suspect in a murder enquiry in one of his rooms, added, "I... I... of course want to help in any way I can."

"I understand that he's not in?" Scott asked.

"No, surprisingly he isn't. Normally he is. My wife hasn't been able to access his room for two weeks. He's left a do not disturb sign on his door and told us in no uncertain terms to stay out, which frankly scared the shit out of me and my wife." He paused before continuing, "He has one of those haunting faces; you can't tell what he's thinking when you look at him. There's no expression, just a blank face."

"Can you let us into the room now, please?"

Burgess led them upstairs. Room three was the first room they came to on the left-hand side of a corridor. He slid a master card into the electronic key slot, and a small green light lit up to confirm entry.

"Mr Burgess, please wait here, and do not enter under any circumstances."

He nodded several times, shifting from one foot to another, trying to glance into the room as the officers entered. Scott closed the door behind them.

"What is that smell?" Raj said as he held his hand over his mouth. "It stinks like the men's bogs at work."

Their attention was drawn towards the likely cause. A pile of black clothing in one corner of the room.

The bedroom itself was like every other B & B bedroom found the length and breadth of the country. The room was dominated by a double bed with an unfashionable pink floral duvet cover that partially hung off the edge of the unmade bed. A winged brown armchair sat in another corner that had seen better days, and a TV and tea-making facilities sat on the chest of drawers by the window.

The room looked untidy. The musty smell suggested it hadn't been ventilated in weeks.

As Scott glanced around, what he saw confirmed they'd found the final bits of the jigsaw.

Scattered around the floor were old press articles about the death of Stephen Wentworth. There was a large street map of Brighton pinned to the wall. Whilst Raj checked out the en-suite bathroom, Scott moved closer to look at the map, whilst Sian looked through the chest of drawers. Scott could see the Urban and Phoenix nightclubs circled, together with the residential addresses of all three victims.

"Guv, there's a towel with what looks like bloodstains on it." Raj pointed over his shoulder as he reappeared from the bathroom.

"Any sign of a knife?" Scott asked, looking around the room.

Raj shook his head, Sian confirming its absence too, but pointed to a black hoodie folded in the top drawer.

"Our suspect's hoodie, guv?" she suggested.

Scott pursed his lips in frustration as he continued scanning the room.

The silence was broken by Scott's radio crackling with static and bursting into life.

"Guv, officers have spotted someone nearby matching the description. He saw the patrol car and legged it. They're in pursuit, and we're behind them." The urgency in Mike's voice matched his rapid commentary.

"It's our man," shouted Scott as he ran for the door, almost knocking Burgess over, the others a few steps behind. Taking a few steps at a time, Scott ran to the car, shouting at Raj to drive.

As they joined the pursuit, Scott radioed for backup. "DI Baker here. We're in pursuit of a suspect. He's potentially armed and dangerous. Request an ARV to make its way to the area."

The radio controller replied that the nearest firearms officers were six minutes away. Scott cursed. It would all be over before they got there.

42

The man panicked like a trapped animal and kept officers at bay as he screamed and waved his knife wildly before disappearing into the cemetery car park and the buildings behind it. The situation had been contained by the time the wail of sirens tore the air, support converging on the cemetery in Mill Lane from all directions. Mike puffed hard as he clung to the gates, whilst Abby coordinated a containment area.

"Where is he?" Scott asked as he peered down the driveway that led from the road to the burial grounds.

"He ran into the cemetery grounds and to the right, behind the fencing. The other exits are covered, so he must still be there." Mike huffed, trying his hardest to catch his breath, sweat beading off his forehead, his shirt clinging to his chest.

Scott took off his suit jacket and threw it into the boot of his car before putting on his black stab vest.

"Guv?" Mike looked alarmed.

He ignored the concern and began a slow walk down the driveway.

"Guv, what are you doing?" Mike shouted over the wailing sirens. "Armed response will be here shortly, a helicopter is ten minutes away, and so is the DCI. Harvey will kill you if you head in there without backup."

"In ten minutes he could be over the wall at the back and gone," Scott shouted over his shoulder, ignoring the warning. He knew he'd face a disciplinary whether it went well or not. But he needed a peaceful resolution right now, not in a few hours after police mediators had created a tense stand-off, or worse, the suspect had been shot by armed officers.

In truth, Scott needed this resolved his way. The case had played on his mind since day one. He was damned if it was going to be taken out of his hands and resolved with a bullet or, worse still, the suspect taking his own life, leaving Scott without answers.

The air around him stilled. No matter how busy the city streets were around the cemetery, the burial grounds always had an atmosphere of their own. Peace and tranquillity transcended the lives of the living, offering those who had left the world a deserved level of respect.

As he passed through the car park, he heard the faint sob of what he thought was a child. As Scott peered around the corner of a building, he saw a man huddled on the ground, his arms protectively wrapped around his bent legs, his head buried in his knees.

The suspect stiffened and thrust out his knife in defence, his teeth clenched tight, his breath laboured.

Sirens wailing around them only alarmed the suspect further. To reassure him, Scott held his hands out in front of him. "I'm not here to hurt you; I just want to make sure you're okay."

The suspect's eyes were wide, consumed with fear, his hair matted wet from grease and sweat, his black clothes crumpled and dirty.

Finally, he spoke in a soft broken voice. "He's gone... he's gone." Tears escaped from the corners of his eyes.

"It's Nathan, isn't it?" Scott asked gently. "Nathan Taylor?"

The man looked up but said nothing.

"I know... I know what's happened, Nathan. I know about Stephen and your mum. I'm sorry, but they wouldn't have wanted this for you."

"How the hell would you know what they wanted?" Nathan screamed. "He was my brother; he was my only family." Spittle erupted from his mouth, mixing with the salty tears that rolled off his chin.

Scott flicked between maintaining eye contact and evaluating how tight a grip Nathan had of the large survival knife he was waving around. Though the knife had been talked about many times during the last two weeks, Scott was taken aback by its size. It was huge, almost the length of his forearm. He was in no doubt as to why it had been chosen to kill the three men.

"Why did you do this, Nathan? Why put yourself through this?"

"They killed him, they all did, they didn't care about him, they were greedy for money... his money... They poisoned him and hurt him," he spat out as he cradled his head in his hands. His shoulders shook as great sobs racked his body.

Scott crouched down. What struck him was how this man's persona could switch in milliseconds from a grown man to that of a young child, consumed with the same grief as if they'd lost their favourite toy.

Silence prevailed for a few moments before Nathan sobbed and spoke. "It wasn't meant to be like this. I thought getting rid of those bastards would serve justice for Stephen." His eyes met Scott's. "I was getting them back for him."

Scott saw the emptiness and desolation in the man's face, yet there was nothing he could say to make Nathan feel better. He'd lost a brother, a loved one, in the same way that Scott had lost his wife and young, precious child. Nothing could shake the darkness that accompanied grief. For a brief moment he felt empathy for the killer.

"Nathan, why don't you come with me? You need some help, and that's available to you if you just put down your knife and come with me."

Nathan shook his head. "What's the point? You'll only tell me off like all the other men have done. Wherever I went, they told me off and hurt me." His voice was a fraction louder than a whisper.

"No one's going to tell you off. We just want you to be safe."

"I'm going to prison for a long time, aren't I?" His voice was steely and focused as he looked at Scott.

Again, Scott saw the adult surface momentarily.

"Nathan, that's a discussion for another day. We can't sit here all day. I'd much rather go somewhere else where we can talk, and you can tell me all about it. Come with me now before it gets out of hand and someone else gets hurt... What do you say, mate?"

Nathan looked at Scott for what felt like minutes.

The sound of rotor blades whipped the air overhead and captured Nathan's attention. He took a deep breath and stared wide-eyed at the sky.

Scott looked angrily towards the sky when he noticed a change in Nathan, but continued, "What do you say? Don't let Stephen's death be in vain."

Nathan shook his head and scrambled to his feet, keeping Scott at bay as he jabbed the knife in his direction. He continued to glance towards the sky. The helicopter came into view, its rotary blades cutting through the air, sending pulses of noise towards the ground that reverberated through his body.

Fear twisted Nathan's features. He looked around and made a run for it, weaving erratically through the headstones, leaping over plots and kicking over flowers in his wake.

"We've got a runner!" Scott screamed as he headed off in pursuit, unsure how far behind was his backup.

Nathan stumbled in long grass and crashed to the ground before getting up. Scott caught up and lunged. Nathan sidestepped the attempt.

Scott rolled a few times and clipped his shoulder on the corner of a granite kerbed memorial. He landed on his back, and shock waves of pain raced down his side. Winded, he paused a moment, then steadied himself before he rose. He could see Nathan making his way towards a gap in the fence that was sealed off by officers, who now joined in the pursuit.

Scott knew that Nathan had little chance of escape, as all exits were covered, and they had aerial coverage too. The sound of a barking dog somewhere behind confirmed the presence of a police dog on scene.

Nathan doubled back as officers spread out. They closed in on all four sides, causing him to panic more. Blood-curdling screams tore from his throat like he was a wounded animal.

Scott saw the sheer panic and terror etched on Nathan's face as he fell again, his face now bleeding from an impact with the edge of a headstone. Nathan rose to his knees, the knife still in one hand.

Scott sensed the fight draining from Nathan's eyes, the look of surrender washing over him, as his shoulders dropped, and his chest heaved.

He stood slowly, dropping the knife as he did, his body offering no resistance. Scott reached to the back of his trousers and pulled out his rigid handcuffs. He was still fully expecting some resistance as he stepped behind Nathan, pulling both hands behind and securing the cuffs.

“Nathan Taylor, you’re under arrest on suspicion of the murders of Edward Stone, Dave Fraser and Peter Tomlins. You do not have to say anything, but it may harm your defence if you do not mention, when questioned, something which you later rely on in court. Anything you do say may be given in evidence.”

Nathan kept his head bowed, lost in his own sadness, as he was led away to the awaiting swell of officers.

43

Coffee@33 was Cara's favourite place in Brighton to grab a latte and chill for a bit, and Scott could see why. Cosy sofas that swallowed you up, trendy wall art and the heady aroma of coffee beans drifted around them.

"You did well in the end," she commented, slowly stirring the decorative pattern in her latte away.

Scott sighed. "I got there in the end, but shit, the DCI tore a strip off me. She could have thrown the book at me, and I'd now be doing what they are." He nodded in the direction of the waitressing staff behind the counter. "Mind you, she told me, 'The end justified the means,' so I took a rap on the knuckles, and she took the glory."

Cara listened.

"To be honest, I felt a bit sorry for him."

"How come?"

"I examined Stephen's death in more detail. I looked up births and deaths to begin with and focused on his mum. From social services reports, it was evident she ran away from the boys' dad because she was pregnant with twins. She never told him about it, so as far as he knew, she was expecting only one child."

Scott paused and took a sip of his now cold cappuccino.

"She went back to her parents in Reading for a while before returning to Brighton but couldn't cope with the prospect of raising two children, so one was taken into care. That was Nathan, and Stephen was given up for adoption when she couldn't cope with him either."

"Ah, okay, so how did Nathan find out about Stephen?" Cara asked.

"Well, Nathan went from care home to care home, suffered traumatic and sustained abuse, and when he was old enough, went in search of his family."

Cara grimaced, probably at the thought of what Nathan had gone through.

Scott continued, "He found out from social services that his mother had passed away through an overdose. He was informed that he was a twin, so he went looking for his brother. He snooped around, asked in the pubs and clubs, but didn't get anywhere. Stephen had been adopted, had a good upbringing, but had a different surname, so Nathan never found much."

The boy's plight clearly touched Cara.

"Anyway, word got back to Stubbins that Nathan had been sniffing around the clubs looking for his brother. This gave Stubbins the ideal opportunity to get Nathan to do his dirty work for him and get rid of the competition. Stubbins's brother, Luke, visited him on five separate occasions using a false identity. Stubbins instructed his brother to track down Nathan and tell him that it was Stone, Fraser and Tomlins who were responsible for his death, with Tomlins delivering the final blow."

Cara's eyes widened.

"Luke taunted Nathan, told him that the three men were greedy for more business and kept offering Stephen more drugs for twenty quid a pop. It seemed that twenty quid could get Stephen anything he wanted. Luke kept waving a wad of twenty-pound notes in front of Nathan to rile him. That was enough to send Nathan over the edge. He was already unbalanced, and they exploited that weakness in him."

Scott paused and reflected on how easy it was to exploit the vulnerable.

He continued, "As far as Nathan was concerned, he'd lost the last chance of having any family. Stuffing twenty-pound notes in his victim's mouths was his way of saying, 'My brother was worth more than a few twenty-pound notes.'"

"And that explains the hair fibre analysis results… twins. They'd have the same DNA profile," she added.

"Yes. Luke was on the door the night Stephen was hit. Stephen's black hoodie was left behind, and Luke hung on to it. Rather fortunate to be honest. He gave it back to Nathan with a whole sob story about the only memory of his brother, blah-blah… and Nathan wore the hoodie, as he put it, 'to be close to his brother'. They manipulated him right until the end."

"Poor bloke, I know he's committed multiple murders, but I kinda feel sorry for him," Cara offered.

"If I'm honest, I do too. His upbringing was completely different from Stephen's. He was damaged goods by the time he left the care system, and this was the final nail in the coffin. Any chance of normality gone. I'm not condoning his actions by any means, but life dealt him a shit hand," Scott said, shaking his head.

He took a sip of his coffee and stared out the window. "Sadly, Nathan, and to an extent Stephen, were nothing more than pawns in a dirty battle for supremacy in the drugs scene… that's the callous extent of this case. The only winner in all of it is Stubbins."

"So what happens next, Scott?"

"Well, we've only interviewed Nathan with an appropriate adult from social services. The next thing is to get a mental health assessment organised. Social believe he has a mental age of between fourteen to sixteen, and I have to agree to some extent. When I was talking to him, it was like he had a dissociative identity disorder. One minute he was thinking and talking like a kid; the next he showed signs of being a mature adult."

"What, like a split personality?" Scott could see the morbid curiosity igniting in her.

"I would think so, yes… We may never get a conviction in the end – he might not be deemed fit to stand trial. I could see the defence team putting that one forward."

"So what will happen?"

"Secure mental unit or hospital possibly." He paused as he stared into his cup. "Another institution."

"Shit… after all that effort on your part."

"Don't forget the rest of the team… oh, and of course you. Your thoughts about the Mafia and the money marker put us on the right track. So thank you."

Cara smiled. "Just doing my job. Give me a corpse and I'm a happy bunny."

"You bloody weirdo," Scott teased, shaking his head. "Well, anyway, I couldn't have done it without you, so thank you on behalf of Sussex Police."

She laughed and tossed her hair back. "That sounded like an Oscar acceptance speech."

Scott smiled as he watched pedestrians dodge each other on the narrow pavement. In the darkness of the past few weeks, the stories of human tragedy had stretched his abilities as an officer, but there had been one ray of light: he'd discovered how to laugh again. It was all due to the person sitting opposite him.

He smiled. *I owe you one, Cara.*

WE HOPE YOU ENJOYED THIS BOOK

If you could spend a moment to write an honest review on Amazon, no matter how short, we would be extremely grateful. They really do help readers discover new authors.

ALSO BY JAY NADAL

TIME TO DIE

(Book 1 in the DI Scott Baker series)

THE STOLEN GIRLS

(Book 2 in the DI Scott Baker series)

ONE DEADLY LESSON

(Book 3 in the DI Scott Baker series)

IN PLAIN SIGHT

(Book 4 in the DI Scott Baker series)

Printed in Great Britain
by Amazon

27602765R00128